ADDICTED TO
Midnight

ADDICTED TO Midnight
The Straight and Narrow

Chrystal V. Hollins

Addicted to Midnight: The Straight and Narrow
Copyright © 2019 by Chrystal V. Hollins. All rights reserved.

No part of this publication may be reproduced, stored in a retrieval system or transmitted in any way by any means, electronic, mechanical, photocopy, recording or otherwise without the prior permission of the author except as provided by USA copyright law.

This novel is a work of fiction. Names, descriptions, entities, and incidents included in the story are products of the author's imagination. Any resemblance to actual persons, events, and entities is entirely coincidental.

The opinions expressed by the author are not necessarily those of URLink Print and Media.

1603 Capitol Ave., Suite 310 Cheyenne, Wyoming USA 82001
1-888-980-6523 | admin@urlinkpublishing.com

URLink Print and Media is committed to excellence in the publishing industry.

Book design copyright © 2019 by URLink Print and Media. All rights reserved.

Published in the United States of America

ISBN 978-1-64367-558-9 (Paperback)
ISBN 978-1-64367-557-2 (Digital)

1. Fiction
2. Christian Romance
26.06.19

The Road is Wide but Narrow Is the Path

"Enter ye in at the strait gate: for wide is the gate, and broad is the way, that leadeth to destruction and many there be which go in thereat: because strait is the gate and narrow is the way, which leadeth unto life and few there be that find it"

-St. Matthew 7:13-14, KJV

Chapter One

David met Lyla at the Golden Capri hotel, when Lyla left her ex-boyfriend Benjamin. She was going through a hard time. Her father fired her from his firm, her boyfriend cheated on her with her best friend and Nina had become the enemy.

She couldn't accept the idea of her father firing her, but being angry at Benjamin and Nina for what they had done made perfect sense. Lyla deserved better. Her father, Albert Johnson was a very busy man. Pastor of the Pure of Heart Baptist Church and the owner to one of the largest firms in Brooklyn, Albert's hands were busy with his work schedules and other responsibilities. Albert needed people who were willing to be corporative and respectable to him but Lyla didn't follow up.

She was deeply influenced by the world's embrace that she'd forgotten about the morals of respect and corporation. As she sat in the loud golden yellow taxi, she replayed the last conversation that she had with her father. After recovering from her injuries, she wanted to celebrate. Lyla had invited all her friends including Nina, when they were close at the time. What followed afterwards was unexpected as Benjamin arrived with his arms crossed with Nina's as they entered into the room. The party had mostly girls and two other guys.

The guys were some friends of Benjamin. What a night! She waited for everyone to leave to clean up, when her father came home in full rage. Once everyone left, the real party began when her father's voice shook the house.

"As long as you are under my roof, you will abide by my rules," he said pointing his finger in her face making him clear about the matter.

"Then maybe I should leave," she said. "I wasn't giving you anything, but a headache anyway," she rolled her eyes and showed rebellion.

"That is completely up to you, but if you leave now, you cannot come back. I will not allow such sinful living in my house. And you could forget about coming back to the firm, young lady. Your attitude is unacceptable," he said shaking his head in disapproval.

Then I'd go," she said as she gathered her belongings.

Now she sat in the backseat of a musty yellow taxi, while her mind pondered on life. She had been very disrespectful to her father for no reason at all. She needed to get away, she had become a prisoner to her own lust. As she closed her eyes, the taxi driver took her far away into a neighborhood that appeared strange to her. Blinded by the pouring rain, she felt like she had gone into another world, a place where everything looked new. She had never been here before.

The hotel sign said: **Golden Capri**.

Could she afford to stay here? With only a hundred and fifty-five dollars to her name, Lyla was broke with no money. She didn't know what to do or where to go. Hoping she would find somewhere to lay her head with kind people around, she walked into the Golden Capri hotel to find a room. Her creamy-white blouse was soaked from the rain outside and her black slacks were ripped down the bottom. Lyla looked like a famous movie star playing a role of a *running* away child, because she looked very beautiful in spite of being drenched.

Her brown hair fell from her face to her back as she swirled around looking for some kind of assistance.

"Hello, how may I help you?" a woman behind the front desk asked. She looked around Lyla's age, in her mid-twenties. She was tall and pretty with curly black hair. Her name tag read: Valerie. She repeated the question again to make sure that Lyla heard her, but this time she included her name.

"Hello, I'm Valerie. How may I help you?"

"Hi, my name is Lyla and I need a room to stay in," replied Lyla.

"All right. Do you have reservations ma'am?" asked Valerie as she tapped on the mouse under her palm.

"No. I am just walking in."

"Okay. So you are a new guest checking in. Would you like a single or double bedroom?" asked Valerie typing information into the computer.

"Excuse me? I just need a single bedroom. It's only me," said Lyla looking at Valerie strangely. *Why would she asked me that? Doesn't she see that I am the only guest here in this lobby?"* thought Lyla confused. Being an attendant at the desk, it was Valerie's job to ask the guests for either a single or double bedroom, when staying inside. But Lyla wouldn't know the procedures, because she never been there.

Chapter Two

"The single bedrooms were $130.00 to $205.00 a night depending on the room's location and the double bedrooms were $210.00 to $280.00 night depending on the room's space," said Valerie professionally. "May I see some identification and would you like to pay with cash or credit?"

"Are you serious? For a single bedroom it cost one hundred and thirty dollars to two hundred and something dollars?" asked Lyla. "Wow!"

When Lyla was working, spending one hundred and thirty dollars or more wasn't a big deal because another pay check would be coming soon. But now that her father has fired her and she was given her last pay check, she tried to spend wisely and buy the things she really needed like this hotel room.

"Well if possible can I get a single bedroom that is no more than one hundred and twenty dollars but less than two hundred and ten dollars in a smaller location on the second or third floor?" asked Lyla.

"I think so let me check the records on the computer. There is a single bedroom located on the second floor. The location is average and the space is small." said Valerie as she scanned the computer.

"Yes. I will take that room. How much does that room cost?" asked Lyla.

"The room cost one-hundred and forty-five dollars. That room has a special today, because of the small room space," said Valerie. "So call it a blessing that you've got the room."

"That's great. I'm happy I got the room." *Now if only I had the money.* "Ms. Valerie, I have a confession to make I don't have a lot of money right now but if you let me stay here for a few nights I promise to pay you back for the hotel room," asked Lyla so quickly that the words came out before she could take a breath. Lyla made sure that Valerie heard her plea before shutting her down.

"I do have some money on me, but if I spend it I don't know how I will eat or get the personal things that I will need. I don't have any other place to go and it is pouring outside. But if I have to leave I understand, since I don't have any money," said Lyla sadly as she walked toward the door.

"So how were you going to pay if the room will have cost two hundred and something dollars? I thought that you at least had a hundred dollars." said Valerie with the concern. "If you would have told me earlier, we could have saved time."

"I know, but what do you say now?" asked Lyla "Can I stay or do you want me to leave?" Being hesitate, Valerie didn't know what to do. She hardly knew this woman to be giving her any special privileges and yet she felt a sense of sympathy for the poor woman. So Valerie decided to let Lyla stay at the hotel.

"Well...I usually don't do this, but you seem like a person in need, so I am willing to let you stay here until you get the money to pay for your room." said Valerie. "It would have been rude to ask you to leave in this pouring rain, so I would try to speak with my supervisor to see what he would say about this," said Valerie.

"Thank you so much. I will pay you back as soon as possible. Thank you again," said Lyla with gratitude. The room is on the second floor, room #203.

"This is the room that you've asked for earlier," said Valerie.

Someone had spilled some milk on the stairs carrying a lingering odor in the hallway, so Valerie suggests taking the elevators.

"Please excuse the mess. I'll clean it up soon. I just have been so busy." Taking the elevators, Lyla's room seem to be only a five minute walk down the hallway by the Jacuzzi and the snack machine on the first floor. The hallway was long and narrowed with velvet carpeting and white plastered wall. Settling into the room, Lyla put a few picture frames on the small bed night stand of her dogs. She still couldn't believe it.

Chapter Three

The next morning, Lyla woke up around seven o'clock with a grumpy attitude. She wasn't use to waking up alone without seeing her man beside her. It made her feel uncomfortable. But that's what happen when Lyla winds up in a fight with her man. She slept and woke up alone, but when she saw Charlie and Miley smiling in the pictures she got a sense of some joy, yet she was still upset about that. She didn't remember what they were fighting about exactly; she said over and over again to forget the scars that he left imprinted on her heart. The TV was on from last night, playing re-runs of who knows what, while Lyla took a long shower and washed her hair.

The hot steam from the shower floated in the air, when she stepped out to dry off. Her hair was dripping wet when she wrapped it up. It was Saturday morning and the sun was shining brightly. A glimpse of the sun light covered the room through the rotating blinds. Drying off, Lyla put on her pajamas that Benjamin bought her when they were together. Wearing the pajamas, stirred up old feelings about him. She was beginning to miss him.

She wondered why she put on those pajamas, *whatever happened to her Betty Bop pajamas*? She searched through her bag to find them. She hoped Nina didn't take them. If she did, this would not be the first thing that she had took from Lyla. Nina was always jealous of her. *Why?* Lyla didn't know and left too soon to find out. Lyla just needed some time alone.

She knew that if she would have ignored the past, that she would only leave room for resentment in her heart. But she didn't know how to face it. She could pray, but what would she say to Him? Her life was full of skeletons, that she trembled before Him. Still Nina could have taken her pajamas; only the Lord knows. Lyla put her hair in a ponytail before leaving the room. She wore her red ruby robe and black slippers.

Grabbing the room key, Lyla closed the door behind her. As she walked down the hallway, the smell of smoked bacon, sausage, eggs, waffles, pancakes floated in the air coming from the lobby. "Mmm…that smells good, Lyla said as she sniffed the air. "*I need to go downstairs now* thought Lyla. Breakfast was being served in the lobby. As Lyla walked, she reached the end of the line that was very long. Twenty people were already in the line waiting to be helped.

A few of them looked familiar. Lyla saw Valerie and a handsome guy standing beside her. His name tag read: Joseph. Both were welcoming the guest into the breakfast area. "Good morning, Valerie. Hey boy," Lyla said as she waved to Valerie and the guy. He was attractive with broad shoulders, brown eyes and a cute smile. His complexion was caramel with Indian hair. He resembled one of those male characters that were in those action movies. Good looking.

"Lyla, I would like for you to meet my husband Joseph," said Valerie as Lyla's eyes slowly moved up and down at him.

"Oh, it is so nice to meet you." Lyla shook Joseph's hand. "The pleasure is all mine," responded Joseph.

The line had decrease some, so now there were only ten people. *What is taking them so long?* Lyla was ready to eat. She hope that there would be some food left by the time she got inside. The line began to move. "Thank God!" The line was moving faster. There were only three people left waiting to go in. The three people were a woman with her daughter, an elderly woman with her grandson, and Lyla.

"Good morning, we have two empty seats in the back corner," Valerie assured the first guests as she pointed to the direction.

"Thank you," responded the mother as she grabbed her daughter's hand. The elderly woman smiled at Valerie as she came near the entrance and gave her a hug.

"Good morning, Mrs. Golden. How are you this morning?" asked Valerie. "I am blessed child and highly favored. How are you and Joseph?"

"We're fine. We are happy to see you this morning. And how are you, Mr. Strong Man?" Valerie asked Thomas, her grandson. "Are you still lifting weights?"

"I need to stay fit for the ladies," responded Thomas.

"I know that's right," giggled Valerie as she gave Thomas a hi-five.

"Finally, I am the last one." shouted Lyla. "Hey Valerie, how are you? Are there any more seats for me?" asked Lyla as she grabbed her plate and looked around. "Well, it looks like we have a few available seats, make your choice," responded Valerie.

"Alright, thanks girl," said Lyla.

"You're welcome. No problem," responded Valerie.

Inside the breakfast room, the place was packed. There were people everywhere. Toddlers to children and teens to adults, Lyla would have never thought that a small hole like this could hold so many people. "Well the breakfast must be a buffet, because there are so many people to have a personal waiter assist them," said Lyla as she glanced around the room. She still couldn't believe it.

Chapter Four

Breakfast was served as a buffet, so that all guests might help themselves. Lyla grabbed two plates, just in case she ran out of room on the first plate and began to fill them. On the first plate, Lyla had some scrabble eggs, three sausage patties, two French toast and a scoop of hash brown. On the second plate, she had two pancakes one waffle and a mixed fruit cup. Before Lyla could get something to drink, she found a table and sat down.

She found a table by the window. "Perfect!" *Now if someone could help her with those plates.*

"Hey Valerie, can you help me carry these plates?" asked Lyla, balancing herself.

"Sure, do you know where you're sitting at?" asked Valerie as she helped Lyla with her plates.

"Yes. I am planning on sitting at that table by the window," said Lyla pointing toward the table.

"Oh, I see," said Valerie. The table was across from Mrs. Golden and her grandson, Thomas.

"Yeah, I guess." said Lyla. She didn't know Mrs. Golden that well. Valerie helped Lyla with her plates, Valerie walked to the table and placed the plates down.

"Here you go. Is there anything else you need?" asked Valerie.

"No, thank you," said Lyla adjusting the chair as she sat down.

"You are welcome," said Valerie before walking away. Lyla positioned her plate before getting her apple juice. She decided to get one glass instead of two, to make more room for her breakfast. Retuning back to the table with her apple juice, Lyla said her grace and began to eat. As Lyla ate her breakfast, she looked across the table to see Mrs. Golden.

She looked like a kind woman who was about sixty-four or five years old, with white peppered hair and blue eyes. She wore a turquoise turtle neck sweater and a pair of black pants. As she ate her breakfast, her grandson stared at Lyla with bulked eyes. She wondered why he stared at her like that. She didn't want to start anything, but she felt very uncomfortable. The little boy continued to stare at her. *What is his problem?*

"Thomas, stop staring at that woman and eat your breakfast, before your food gets cold," his grandma said. Lyla was happy to see his grandma taking care of the problem. Lyla continued to eat and tune them both out.

"But grandma, I am not hungry. Grandma, do you know who that woman is over there?" he asked pointing his small index finger at Lyla.

"No, but I do know she is eating her breakfast like you need too," responded his grandma.

"It's Lyla Star!" exclaimed the young boy.

"Lyla who? Who is Lyla Star?" asked the grandma.

"She is Lyla Star! The woman who is sitting across from us. You know the inspirational talk show host and radio speaker that use to come on every morning around nine-thirty?" asked Thomas.

"I don't believe this. Thomas why are you calling people names? I told you that is not polite," said the grandma.

"But, grandma I am not calling people names. That is Lyla Star! Grandma Golden still didn't believe Thomas, so she grabbed her wooden cane and walked toward the young woman. Thomas had done enough talking about this girl. The time had come for her to see if it was her. As she walked closer, Lyla gathered her disposables and stood up to stretch.

"Good morning, are you Lyla Star?" asked the woman as she balanced herself on her cane.

"Excuse me?" Lyla was startled by the woman's presence.

"Are you Lyla Star?" asked the woman again.

"Yes. Who wants to know?" replied Lyla gently.

"Oh my," the grandma cried. She couldn't believe it. "You're Lyla Star? The one who speaks at those conferences across town, spreading the good news? God bless you," said the grandma.

"And you are?" Lyla asked the elderly woman.

"My name is Samantha, Samantha Golden." said the woman.

"Nice to meet you, Samantha. But I do not speak at those conferences anymore nor do I travel. Now, I just live my life like normal people," responded Lyla. "Sorry".

"It's all right. I guess everybody falls one day or another. I just wished you hadn't fallen so soon. Hopefully, you would get back out there again. I really missed hearing your encouraging words on the radio and television. You don't know how much joy you gave me when I saw a young woman like yourself working for the Lord. Well, you take care now and have a blessed day, "said the woman as she held Thomas hand and exit the room.

Chapter Five

On Sunday morning, Lyla felt icky and dirty inside, like she haven't bathed in weeks. Lyla could not shake those words off. What did Samantha meant, when she said "I guess everybody falls one day or another." Was Samantha encouraging her or talking about her? She knew that she had done some bad things in her life, but haven't everyone? Nobody was perfect.

She knew she had slipped a few times, but never had she fallen down and stayed. We all fall down and make mistakes. What was so different about her failures and mistakes? Why did it seem like everyone was upset and disappointment at her? In spite of the way she looked, Lyla still felt empty. On the outside nobody could see her true emotions, but inside she bled. Being the type of person that she was, she would have ignored Mrs. Golden's words and woke up happy.

But those were some powerful words "*I guess everybody falls one day or another...*" What had caused Lyla to fall in the first place? Life! Life! Life! Life made Lyla fall: the influences, the environment, the whole atmosphere, the people, the drama, the abuse, the betrayal, the hurt. Lyla began to cry.

Lyla missed her old life, when she was happy and smiling. Doing the right thing and staying positive. *What happened to that*? She stared up at the ceiling. Being all worked up, she quickly changed the words around as a defense. *Forget what Samantha says.* Nothing was wrong with Lyla. Something was wrong with her. How dare she say that Lyla had a problem in the most polite way? Lyla hadn't fallen she did.

All worked up now, Lyla felt a little bit better. She had to learn how to not feel sorry for herself. She hated to feel sad and upset about foolish things. Stretching Lyla got up and went to the bathroom. She turned the shower knob for hot water and removed her clothes. As Lyla stood in the shower, she allowed the water to wash all the filth that clung to her body. *Wouldn't that be nice, if she could remove every pain from her body by taking a shower?* Maybe the pain will soon be over.

Turning on the television, Lyla flipped through the channel until she heard a familiar voice of a woman she once knew. This woman on the television was very beautiful. She had curly hair and wore a white blouse with a khaki skirt. She was smiling and happy. Looking good and feeling good, doing the right thing and staying positive. The woman on the television was saying the words, "I am special and loved and so are you. I deserve respect and should…Lyla turned off the television before the woman finished her words and began to say the rest of the sentence. "I deserve respect and should not be misused or abused, but cherish like a precious rose."

After all these years, Lyla still remembered those words from a long time ago. Those were the words that Lyla would write down and say everywhere when she was in the ministry. She missed that woman so much. She used to encourage her when she needed it. Lord, she would do anything to see that woman face to face again. She would do anything to feel her joyous presence. The reason why Lyla was so in love with this woman on the television was because of their identical identity. Both were beautiful and intelligent women, but one had passed away.

The woman that was outside of the television had passed away. The beautiful woman that was on the television show was Lyla Star, when she was spreading the Word. The show took place a few years ago, when she was nineteen years old. Now she was twenty-three. "Wow!" She was a young little thing. She didn't know that these old conferences came on TV. She thought they were over, when she stopped. Guess she was wrong. Watching the hourly talk show of hers brought back so many memories, when she used to be the sweetest girl in the world with a loving spirit.

Chapter Six

Every Sunday she would go to church faithfully and participate in the choir. She was one of a kind, always smiling and happy. Many people were inspired and wanted to be like her. She had this confidence in her like any other that made her stand out of the crowd and shine. She was an inspirational speaker that spoke at women's conferences. While attending these conferences, Lyla encouraged many women in building up their self-esteem.

She have been called a life saver or an angel because she would breakdown some walls of hatred within many women by telling them that God loves them, God is love and that love should be shown in their lives. She use to always say "Everyone needs to see a caring heart and loving spirit once in a while and we as women should play that part". Lyla also spoke to young men and encouraged them as well. Every time Lyla spoke to them she made sure they knew where she was coming from as a woman.

As a speaker, she would develop some kind of relationship with them, so that they would be able to accept and understand each other. But God is so good, he already worked it out. Now all she had to do was be obedient. However, it was still easier to talk to women because women were more gentle hearted, but with the men she came prepared and strong.

She was recognized by everyone: from the conferences to church, from the church to the public. Everyone admired her characteristics as a leader and motivator.

She was asked by many church administrators to speak at that church and this church like a movie star. Many people wanted to hear an encouraging word from Lyla that would lift up their spirit. But that was a few years ago, now Lyla was in the position of someone else telling her the good news or even a nice word. Lyla had never felt so alone in her life. She had lost her job, her condo, her man, her dignity as a woman. But that was the past, today was the present. Changing the subject, she wondered what kind of breakfast was being served downstairs.

She could still feel the hurt and pain that she experienced when she was in a relationship with Benjamin. She began to think about something else to spare the tears. *Whatever was cooking smelled pretty good* as she sniffed the air. The aroma was coming from the lobby. She wondered who was doing the cooking, perhaps one of those skilled chiefs. She could taste a breakfast omelet with steak and mozzarella cheese. *Those are the best omelets* she said, skipping happily down the hall to the lobby.

As Lyla walked through the lobby, she noticed a man wearing a fine stitched black suit. He stood behind the front desk looking at some paperwork. He looked very sharp with his black gator shoes and handsome. *He was fine. Hey boy what's your name?* Lyla walked toward the front desk.

"Hey, Dave how are you?" asked Valerie coming in from her walk.

"Oh, I am doing well. I am just reviewing some paper work. How's Joseph?" he asked before heading outside to leave.

"He is good, just busy working," responded Valerie before drinking from her water bottle. She took a long sip. "Hey Lyla. I didn't recognize you there."

"Hey Valerie," responded Lyla staring at the man leaving the lobby. "Who is that?"

"Oh, that's David Stokes, the owner of this hotel." said Valerie.

"He is fine! Is he single? Is he married? Does he have kids? How good is his credit?" asked Lyla rapidly without taking a single breath.

"Slow down with the questions, Lyla. First get to know him," said Valerie patiently. "David is single. He doesn't have any children and has never been married before. About his credit, the last time I heard it was nice and he is a gentleman." said Valerie.

"And how do you know so much about David?" asked Lyla. "Did you use to date him or something?" asked Lyla.

"No. I just do my research, asking many questions," responded Valerie. "But if I wasn't married, I would have definitely spoken to him. He is so cute." David Stokes is six-two with board shoulders and firm hands. He was dark skinned with light brown eyes and a cute smile.

"He is drop dead gorgeous. I can't believe he's not married. A woman must be a fool to not hook up with him," said Lyla.

"Would you like to meet him?" asked Valerie before going to her room to change.

"Yes, but first let me fresh up." As she headed upstairs to change, David came back to the lobby.

Chapter Seven

Lyla rushed out of her room that she didn't know what she had worn before going down to the lobby. She had just followed the scent of some good cooking. Looking at herself, Lyla still had on her pajamas and black slippers. *Wow!* She needed to change. Wouldn't that have been embarrassing, she imagined. *Tap, tap, and tap.* "Who is it?" asked Lyla rapidly.

"It's Valerie, can I come in?" asked Valerie adjusting her red polo shirt.

"Not right now. I need to find something to wear for David," responded Lyla.

"Well, David is here beside me and would like to meet you." said Valerie. Knocking things over, Lyla grabbed the knob and yanked the door open. "Whew, hey David…wait where is he?"

"At the front desk," responded Valerie. "I just wanted you to open up the door."

"Why you little…Hush. You better not say it," said Valerie quickly stopping Lyla in the middle of her sentence. She couldn't believe that Valerie had fooled her. As Valerie walked into the room, she saw pictures of two cute puppies on Lyla's night stand, but didn't say anything.

"Well since you are here, can I get your opinion? What do you think of this dress?" asked Lyla, modeling her black strapless dress. "Doesn't this look good?"

"Yeah, for a dinner or something. You're just going downstairs to say hello, that's all." responded Valerie.

"Well, what if I get lucky and he asks me out, shouldn't I be prepared?" asked Lyla professionally, as she looked around the room to find her black heels.

"You know if David would have asked you out, it would be because of your character and your personality, not because of your body features and appearance," said Valerie honestly. Lyla knew that Valerie was right, but she wasn't trying to hear that. Right now she looked good. She sprayed a mist of perfume to complete her look. She looked fabulous! He would have to be a fool to deny her. As she grabbed the room key, Lyla and Valerie left the room and Lyla locked the door. They both walked down the stairs to the lobby.

Chapter Eight

David was looking over some documents, when he saw a pair of legs coming down the stairs. He almost fainted when he saw her. The woman was the woman he had been praying for. The woman on the talk shows, the incredible speaker. Lyla was thrilled to see him behind the desk, watching her as she flipped her hair. Valerie hinted for her to walk over, nudging her arms...*go on*. David contemplated for a moment, he wanted to say hello but was too shy.

He had been a coward to these sorts of things. But he knew that if he didn't say something now, he would have missed the opportunity. He took a deep breath. Lyla fely Valerie tugging her arm, he was waiting. They both walked toward the desk. David inhaled once more and spoke. "Hi, my name is David Stokes and you are?" He said a silent prayer in his head as he waited for her name. She couldn't be the talk show host. Her name cannot be...

"Hello, my name is Lyla Star," said Lyla.

"Nice to meet you, Lyla. That sure is a pretty name," said David leaping with joy on the inside. His prayer had come true.

"Thank you. So what type of job do you have?" asked Lyla.

"Well, here at the Golden Capri hotel, I am the business manager," responded David. "So do you still go to church, Lyla?"

"Pardon me?" *Did he just ask if she went to church? is he a friend of her father?* Lyla was somewhat startled. She turned around to find that Valerie had left her. "I am sorry David. Did you ask me if I went to church?"

"Yes I did. You still go right?" asked David with joy in his eyes.

"Sometimes, when I can. Why do you want to know?" asked Lyla.

"I was just curious. You know if you don't have a church home, you are welcome to come to my church. I go to Pure of Heart Missionary Baptist." said David all friendly. She had a feeling that he would say that church of all churches.

"David, I don't know. Just pray for me, okay." said Lyla slowly walking away from the desk. She had a feeling that he would preach to her next and she wasn't in the mood to hear that now.

"Lyla wait! If you ever decide to go just give me a call. Here is my number," he scribbled his number down on a piece of the hotel's notepad and gave it to her. "Call me anytime" he smiled as she received his kindness.

"Thank you, David," said Lyla.

"You are welcome. I really enjoyed talking to you Lyla, we should definitely do it again some time. Unfortunately, I have to leave now and run a few errands. But just call me whenever I will be by the phone waiting to hear from you," said David with a grin on his face.

"You know I will. Have a blessed day." said Lyla as she waved goodbye. *Wow!* Lyla really felt blessed. Who would have known that a simple conversation would have become the best conversation that she ever had. *Wow!* Is all Lyla could say. She needed more of that, whatever it was. Lyla couldn't put her finger on David. He was like a man that she hadn't met before. Of course, she just met him today but this guy was different. His eyes twinkled when he spoke of church, so anyone could only imagine how his whole face expression might have been when he spoke of the actual Savior.

    He sounded well mannered. Every word that he said was so proper and fluent that he appeared to Lyla as that of a leader or head chief, which was amazing in itself: to know that a man had his priorities in order and was focused. Just a man like that alone, could charm her. Lyla loved it when a man knew what he wanted in life and what he needed to do to get what he wanted. Every man in life wasn't focus just a few were really. She wished Ben would have been more focused on the right things, then the wrong things. Then maybe they could have been together. Why did Benjamin have to hurt her?

Chapter Nine

The pain that Benjamin left behind scarred her deeply. How could someone full of charm be so mean? And how could someone that made her smile, make her cry? She knew that love was supposed to heal not tear down and mend not break, but she guessed she was wrong. Lyla tried to forget the pain that lingered in her heart, but it was too difficult. She loved Benjamin so much. How come he didn't love her? She knew that love went a long way and lust was only temporarily. Come to think of it, the love that she had for Benjamin could have been strong lust, that was why she felt so attached to him.

Lyla was drawn by his features and his physical body that she didn't want to see the wrongs and faults that laid before her. She was so amazed with his charm that she didn't want anything or anyone else but him. But when something seemed too real to be true it was. Staying with Ben revealed unspeakable passion that she couldn't live without, lustful motives that engulfed her so secretly. What was it about Ben that made her thighs tingle and her legs to quiver? She didn't know what it was, but she did know that sex had consequences.

Not even her mind could comprehend this, so it must be that powerful. Being with Ben was amazing, but now Lyla looked for another who could complete her. David would you be that real man? Would you be the one that was heaven sent? David had a style that was persuasive and balanced. Lyla got the impression that David would be the type to give away his worldly possessions for the journey of Christ. Lyla became tired so she headed back to her room.

David was a smart and attractive man. She still couldn't believe that he was single. She pressed the up arrow to the elevators. *Ding.* The elevator door opened up. Lyla walked down the lonely aisle thinking about the conversation she had with David. She couldn't get him out of her mind. It had been a while since Lyla been with a man. As she walked into the room, she could still smell the perfume that she had put on earlier. The soft fragrance put a smile on her face. Removing her dress, Lyla took a nice long shower, because she feared she might sleep in the tub.

Lyla put on some silky pajamas and went to bed. She sat the alarm for nine-thirty A.M. in the morning like she had to be up for work or something and stretched. She said her prayers and closed her eyes. She might not go to church every Sunday, but she still said her prayers every night.

Lyla woke up the next morning with a smile on her face. *Good morning sun, good morning grass. Good morning to everyone!* Lyla was so happy. She had a wonderful dream. This business manager named David Stokes was talking to her about going to church and stuff. He was so polite. Single with good credit, yes David was one of a kind. Before leaving her bed, Lyla said a quick prayer when she heard a knock on the door. *Thump, thump, thump.* "Who is it?" asked Lyla.

"Room service," replied a man's voice.

"Room service? *Who would call room service at nine-thirty in the morning?* Before opening the door, Lyla washed her face and brushed her teeth. There was nothing more embarrassing then having sleep in her eyes and bad breath. As Lyla opened the door, she was surprise to see David. "Hey, how did you get here? I had a dream about you last night. How did you become so *real*?" asked Lyla skeptically. "Have I been pranked?"

"No, Lyla. You just had sweet dreams about me. We met each other last night. I believe I had asked you to church," responded David.

"Oh yeah. Now I remember. So what brings you by this early?" asked Lyla.

"Church. Today is Sunday morning." responded David.

"Okay, that's good. But what does that have to do with me?" asked Lyla.

"Well, I would like for you to come with me. I really think you should." responded David.

"I don't know. I haven't been in church in about two to three years. I would feel weird." said Lyla. "Maybe next Sunday, but not today. I still have my pajamas on." said Lyla. "Sorry."

It's okay, maybe next time. I bought you some breakfast." said David.

"Aw, thank you. You didn't have to do that. You are so sweet." said Lyla.

"You are welcome. I think you are sweet too. Well, enjoy your breakfast." said David.

"Thank you, I will. Have a nice time at church. Don't forget to tell me the message." said Lyla.

"Oh, I will. Have a nice day." said David.

"Thank you." said Lyla. He was so sweet.

Chapter Ten

Lyla placed the breakfast platter on the table and took a bath. Lyla ran the bath water until it reached the top. The water was hot with tons of bubbles. "Ahh, that's feels good," said Lyla as she sat in the tub. The water was perfect. Lyla absorbed every relax ripple of the water, before washing up. She wasn't in a rush to be clean, just at peace. Laying her head on the tip of the tub's rim, her hair flowed in the ripples of the water. Oh, her hair's wet, who cared. Not she. Grabbing a hair band, Lyla banded her hair and began to wash up.

The soap was white lavender. The sponge was navy blue. She caressed her body with the stroking of the sponge touching against her skin. Lyla dried off with a Betty Bop's towel. Her hair had completely dried before her body, so all she had to do was just dry off. She put on a nice white blouse with khaki capris. She walked over to the table with the breakfast platter. *Oh, bless his heart.* Lyla thought that David bought some cereal with milk, a slice of toast and a large glass of orange juice, but Lyla was in for a big surprise.

As she removed the breakfast lid, she was surprised to see the large breakfast "*Oh my! This is a whole breakfast,*" said Lyla. David had bought her some pancakes, sausages, eggs, hash browns, bacon, two slices of toast, one yogurt and a large glass of apple juice. Before eating, Lyla said grace and picked up the silverware to eat. The food was delicious. Lyla was about to go back to bed. She was so full. She made sure to eat everything; nothing was going to be wasted.

After enjoying her breakfast, Lyla grabbed her room key and went downstairs to the lobby. Valerie was behind the desk, talking on the phone when Lyla came down.

"All right, thanks again. Good bye," said Valerie. "Good morning Star! How did you sleep last night?" asked Valerie smirking.

"I slept peacefully. Why do you asked?" asked Lyla.

"Well, I heard that you and David got close last night," said Valerie.

"Yeah we got close, but not sexually. Just as friends. I really think he is a nice guy," said Lyla. "But he is too churchy, if that's even a word."

"What are you talking about Lyla? David is a good man," said Valerie. "What do you mean, he is too churchy? Would you whether have a rough man that disrespects you or a gentleman who cherishes you?" asked Valerie.

"I don't know. I would whether have the gentleman," said Lyla. But she actually missed Ben, the rough guy. She didn't know what she wanted.

"Give David a chance. He really likes you. I have never seen him like anyone more than he likes you," said Valerie.

"Really? Are you serious? You think David really likes me? How can you tell?" asked Lyla.

"I can tell by his body language, his eyes, and his smile. Look how his whole body changes when he is around you, than you will know what I am talking about," said Valerie.

"Really? Well, I need to check that out," said Lyla smiling. "It was nice talking to you, Valerie but I need to handle some business so I have to go." Lyla said that to just get out of the room. She didn't have any money or a vehicle, so where would she leave exactly.

"All right, but before you go. I want to give you my number, call me whenever."said Valerie.

"Okay, thanks Valerie," responded Lyla.

"You are welcome," said Valerie.

Chapter Eleven

Awaken by the cool breeze outside, Lyla grabbed her blanket for warmth. The temperature felt about thirty-two degrees and the sky was cloudy. *What a perfect day to stay in bed.* She rolled over on her back. The television was on from last night, playing re-runs of Seinfeld. Lyla had thrown her clothes on the floor and ordered two small pans of cheese pizza from Pizza Hut with a side of barbeque wings and two emptied Dr. Pepper cans sat on the table, while one can was half opened.

Whenever Lyla woke up, she would have a lot of work to do. The alarm went off. It was 9:15 A.M. in the morning. Every morning, she woke up at about 9:30 A.M. and stretched. *Oh, what is that smell? It smells like hot cheese mixed with barbeque.* She searched around the room and found some air spray. Fully awaken now, Lyla went to the bathroom. She washed her face and brushed her teeth. After brushing her teeth, Lyla turned on the shower and let the water get steamy. She pulled her hair back into a ponytail and removed her clothes.

The water was just right, not to hot and definitely not cold. *Ah, that feels good.* After taking her shower, Lyla put on her robe and left the bathroom. The steam of the shower had fog up the mirror. Lyla knew that her life was so boring, she really missed the past. The smell of cool water lingered throughout the entire bathroom. But the living room still smelled of hot cheese and barbeque wings. She knew there was some air spray around there that she could use. She began to look around the room again.

Downstairs, an old friend of Lyla came inside the hotel to look for her. "Oh, this hotel is nice. The building is large and the room is so clean," said Nina as she walked into the hotel.

They had been friends ever since high school. Nina was beautiful. She wore a slim black dress that revealed a round belly with flat black shoes.

"Excuse me. Can you tell me where Ms. Star's at?" asked Nina talking to Valerie.

"Do you mean Lyla Star?" responded Valerie.

"Yeah, Ms. Lyla Star. Where is she?" asked Nina again searching around the lobby.

"She should be in her room, number 203 on the second floor," responded Valerie.

"Oh, okay. Thank you." said Nina. As she walked up the stairs to get to Lyla's room, she stopped for a moment and rubbed her belly. She didn't know how to tell Lyla this. Meanwhile, Lyla was changing into her grey sweats and white T-shirt not expecting any company. Lyla's room was around the corner on the right. *Thump, thump, thump.* "Lyla are you in there?" asked Nina in a whisper. "A woman at the front desk said that you were." Nina knocked on the door again.

"Who is it?" said Lyla.

"Girl it's me, Nina," she tried to sound enthusiastic. "Will you please open up the door?"

Nina? What was she doing here? After Ben and Lyla had broken up, due to a disturbing image, Lyla had stopped talking to her. She was still upset about what Nina did to her. But Lyla had move on with her life. Whatever Nina and Benjamin did now, it didn't affect Lyla in any way. Yet, she was still surprise to hear Nina's voice.

"Hey Lyla are you going to let me in at all?" asked Nina softly. Lyla was hesitating to open the door. She wished that Nina would have stayed where she was. "I see that you are still looking good," said Nina as she walked toward the bed. Nina stretched her legs out. Lyla stood before her speechless. Again, she wasn't expecting company. She wasn't happy to see Nina at all.

"How did you find me? How did you know where I lived?" asked Lyla.

"By calling several people, when your father told me. Why did you move out here so far away? Why the sudden change?" asked Nina as she motioned herself up out of the bed.

"You should know why, trader!" said Lyla disgustedly.

"Lyla, I didn't come up here to argue with you, but to apologize. Lyla I am so sorry," said Nina.

"How could you hurt me like that?" asked Lyla walking toward the door. "Maybe it's best you leave now."

"Lyla I told you I was sorry. Why are you treating me this way?" asked Nina slowly rising herself from the bed. Before exiting the room, Nina turned to Lyla and asked again for her forgiveness.

"I would think about it Nina. Good bye," said Lyla closing the door. As Nina walked down the hall, she found an elevator and took that instead. She couldn't do anymore walking. When Nina got to the lobby, she was very sad. Valerie noticed her expression and felt compassion for her. Ever since Lyla moved into the Golden Capri, she had been alone and at peace. So when Nina showed up, she didn't know how to act. Nina was probably living well.

She figured that Nina had her own place, car, and a decent job. Nina had always been Ms. Independent. As Nina walked outside, Lyla saw Nina from her window walked to her white BMW, she got rend of the Supreme Cutlass vehicle and opened up the door. She made a U-turn and drove away from the hotel. Lyla admitted that the car was nice. Knowing Nina, she probably got it sometime last year, maybe late November. What she had to do to get it was a mystery. Lyla would know because if she remembered her well like she should, she probably gave that person a taste of pleasure. If anyone knew what she meant. Listening to Nina hadn't always been the best idea.

Chapter Twelve

Come to think of it, that's how Lyla got into this mess with Benjamin in the first place. Listening to Nina and trying to find someone to share her life with, but she was fine the way she was: preaching and praising God. One day, Lyla was asked to give an inspirational word at a women's conference that she was a part of. Lyla was a missionary preaching God's Word. But even a missionary can become tangled in the snare of the enemy.

Lyla began the conference by encouraging the women. "Who is fearfully and wonderfully made? We are! Whenever Lyla was given a passage to talk about, she became very happy because she knew what the scripture meant. The scripture was talking about the significance of being different. The word "fearfully" didn't mean afraid or scared, but extreme in size and bad...unique and different.

When the conference was over, Nina began to say some words that made Lyla wonder about a relationship with a man. Nina had been dating this guy name Steven for about five months and she was very happy with him. She and Steven went out for dinner, to the movies, and even on vacations. They were always active and on that night Steven and Nina were going to Red Lobster for dinner.

He was picking her up in his black Cadillac and Lyla who had seen it all became jealous. Ever since high school Nina would always have a boyfriend, while Lyla would stay lonely. Lyla was tired of it. Lyla wished that she had a date. She wished her man would take her out if she had one. She wondered where Nina found Steven at any ways. She told Lyla on a date chat line. Nina began to explain how it happened.

Nina began her story, "One day I was bored and was surfing the web, when this ad from this chat line called *Black Single Love* had pop-up. On the ad, there were these three shirtless gorgeous men that were dancing around and happy. What the men were dancing about, I didn't know. But I sure was curious about the whole thing. There was this catchy slogan that read "Hope you are ready for the search of your life as you find love on the best site." That was how I remembered the name of the chat line. I signed up, became a member and met Steven. We have so much in common. We both were good looking, we love the Lord, and we didn't mind having a couple of drinks every once in a while. Yes, the Lord was good. You know I still don't understand why you don't have a man. Lyla you are a beautiful person why you are single I don't know. Maybe you should try the *Black Single Love* chat line to find someone."

After hearing that, Lyla should have prayed first, but instead she was persuaded to try something different. The phrases of *finding* a man, *needing* a man and *wanting* a man circled in Lyla's mind. Maybe Nina was right. Why should everyone have a man, but her? Lyla believed that she was attractive and intelligent enough for a man, so why she didn't have one? She wondered if something was wrong with her.

Maybe the Lord was getting her prince ready and wanted her to be patient, but Lord sometimes she got lonely. She knew there was a mate for everyone, it's just that hers hadn't come yet, so she didn't have a choice but to be patient and wait. Nina said, "That Lyla needed to find a good man, other than the Lord."

"Excuse you? What are you trying to say?" asked Lyla.

"Oh, nothing like that. So don't take it personal. I know that God is good. But have you ever wanted a *real* boyfriend or a play mate?" asked Nina.

"No and yes." Lyla would like to have a boyfriend, but not a play mate. She could never be that freaky. And that's what she thought until she met Benjamin. Lyla met Benjamin through the dating chat line that Nina had introduced her to. Lyla had never been on the chat line before, so she was confused about everything. She googled the word "chat line" and over fifteen hundred websites appeared. Amazed and overwhelmed, Lyla called Nina over when she heard a knock at the door. "Who is it?' asked Lyla.

"Nina. Can I come in?" asked Nina opening the door to come inside.

Chapter Thirteen

As Nina walked into the house, she made herself comfortable. The recommended chat line that Nina had suggested for Lyla was the *Black Single Love* chat line that Nina had used to find her man, Steven. Today was Lyla's birthday and she was spending half of her day on the chat line. So Lyla entered in the name of the chat line and was amaze to find photos of people everywhere. There were men in their mid-twenties and late forties.

Some of the photos of the men and women were very presentable and attractive. There were a few photos of Nina that had been posted sometime last month that were nice and pretty. In one photo, Nina wore this black shimmer dress with a hairstyle of jet black curls all over her head, which made her look very beautiful. In her right hand, she held a martini glass with big smiles. Lyla began to wonder how she would look with jet curly hair and a black dress on. Not as beautiful as Nina, but maybe close.

Before Lyla could do anything, she needed to become a member and sign up. "Welcome to the *Black Single Love* chat line. *Hope you are ready for the search of your life as you find love...*" the welcome was so long. Lyla was ready to get this over with. "To become a member, create a username and a password with eight characters, including one number."

Open to any suggestions, Lyla looked at Nina. What should her username be? Maybe her nickname or a friend's name would work out. Lyla thought about it.

She got a name: Sparkle. Lyla really liked things that sparkled and glittered, plus it sounded pretty. Lyla asked Nina for her opinion.

"It is all right, just missing something. I like the name Sparkle, but it sounded to shallow for me. How about Ms. Sparkle spelled as Mizz Sparkl3? What do you think?" asked Nina.

"I like it!" said Lyla. The name was creative.

"So let keep this as your username and you can create your own password," said Nina, feeling very sure of herself. Keeping the name Mizz Sparkl3, Lyla began to create her password. After creating her password, Lyla had to fill out a descriptive form that described her identity and what type of man she was looking for. On one of the description space, there were a total of nine questions that Lyla had to answer.

The first few questions had to do with Lyla identifying herself and the remaining asked about her favorite color, food, movie, and music. These were the ten questions that Lyla was given: **Last name, first name, gender, birthdate, favorite colors, favorite food, favorite movie, favorite type of music, hobbies, and a list of words that describes who you are.**

Last name: Star

First name: Lyla

Her favorite colors were blue and red. Her favorite movie was the Last Dragon. Her favorite type of music were rhythm and blues and Gospel. Her hobbies were teaching, singing and dancing. A list of words that described her: funny, attractive, intelligent, creative, honest, and slim. She had brown eyes, long hair and a pretty smile. After answering all the questions, Lyla submitted her answers and waited for a response.

Five minutes later, a comment pop-up that read: **Thank you for answering the questions above. Shortly, a message will appear to explain what to do next.**

As Lyla waited, another pop-up box appeared, reading: **Due to technical difficulties the browser cannot open at this time. Would you like to End Now or close page?**

Lyla clicked on "close page" and would try again. The second time Lyla signed on the website; the site froze again, so she gave up.

Chapter Fourteen

Several weeks had gone by and Lyla was still alone. She still couldn't believe that she was single. "Nina, why am I single?" asked Lyla. She got on the chat line to find her Mr. Right and still winded up lonely.

"Lyla just be patient. You will find your Mr. Right one day, just wait." said Nina.

Lyla rolled her eyes. She knew that Nina wasn't talking. She wouldn't know what patience was if it would have slapped her in the face. She was always in a hurry. Lyla said a silent prayer. *Sorry Lord, please forgive me.* She was beginning to feel agitated. It's been about three weeks and she still hadn't heard anything from Benjamin. As far as she knew, they were a perfect match with the same things in common, so what is the hold up?

It was Valentine's Day and Nina had another man. Again, she found her man on the chat line. Lyla was still on the hunt for her first guy. "Nina, I don't know how you do it, but I want to know your secret. How do you find your man so quickly through the chat line? I mean here I am still searching and here you are finished. What did you do?" asked Lyla.

"I ask them to meet me somewhere or just follow me at the spot, sometime at a particular place. Then I describe the dress I will be wearing and talk sexy-like to let them know that I'm hot and wait for them to come running. Guys can't resist it, when I talk sexy to them. They become too excited. "That's how I get the job done." said Nina "It works every time."

"Wow! That's smart. I wish I would have thought of that." said Lyla.

"So are you still planning on going to that Valentine's party tonight at church? I think it starts at seven o'clock." asked Nina.

"Girl, I don't know. I really want to, but I'm upset." said Lyla.

"Well you never know, maybe tonight is your lucky night. I have a feeling that you will probably see Benjamin tonight at the Valentine's party. You know God works in mysterious ways." said Nina.

"Yeah, I know. But I just don't feel like going. I'm tired," said Lyla grumpily.

"Oh come on Lyla! It wouldn't be fun without you. I would go as your date so you want be lonely. Can you come please?" begged Nina. Lyla buried her head in the blanket to ignore Nina's stares and pleas. She hated to look at Nina whenever she was wrong, because Nina would have that 'I told you so' expression on her face. Lyla didn't want to stay home and she definitely didn't want to be alone, she just didn't know what to do.

"Lyla, you know I'm right," said Nina. "You know you really want to go to this party."

"Okay, all right. I would go with you. It's Valentine's Day, a holiday that celebrates love," said Lyla.

Chapter Fifteen

"Girl let get ready to party!" shouted Nina. Going into her room, Lyla didn't know what to wear. She had thought about wearing her birthday dress, which was a strapless white dress with turquoise flowers everywhere. But the dress was for a dinner or a special occasion, not for a party. Lyla needed more of a silk and loose dress that showed her curves and features. Nina must have found her dress last night because she was dressed from head to toe. She wore a silky red dress that revealed her curves in every angle.

She dyed her hair red with brown streaks going through it. Nina looked very hot. Lyla still didn't know what to wear. She looked in her closet for a dress that would blow the eyes of a man away, including Nina's eyes since she seems like the one that always did the blowing. If she couldn't find one, maybe she could borrow a dress from Nina. "Oh Nina, do you have a dress that I can borrow, I can't find anything," asked Lyla.

"Let me see. I think so. You're not looking for anything in particular is you?" asked Nina.

"No, just something nice and sexy." said Lyla.

"How about my purple dress with the long split on the side? I think that is sexy for you," said Nina.

After curling the last strand of black hair she had left, Lyla put on some dark brown lipstick and some light purple eye shadow to bring out her eyes. Nina had put on her dark red lipstick in the car and they were off to the Valentine Party. "I hope we didn't dress inappropriate," Lyla said to Nina. "I don't know why my mind is in the gutter," responded Lyla.

"Me either, but hopefully this party be worth the wild," said Nina. "There's nothing wrong with thinking it, you are human remember."

"Yeah, but this event is held inside of a church."

Arriving at the party, the decoration was set beautifully. The theme colors were red, pink, and black. There were balloons on the wall, the round tables were covered and a hug sign read: *Celebrating Love in the Air.*

"Oh, I feel so special," said Lyla "who would have known that such decorations could stir up feelings inside." The feeling of love was definitely in the air.

"Come on girl, let's dance!" said Nina.

"All right, but let me say hello to everyone first," responded Lyla. As Lyla approached some friends and those who had looked familiar to her, Nina headed to the dance floor.

"Hey DJ play something that is funky," said Nina as she moved her body. Nina was ready to party. "Lyla come dance with me. You had said hello to everyone already," said Nina.

"Oh, all right. You know I can't resist dancing. Say, could you turn that up some more?" asked Lyla. The DJ began to turn up the volume of the speakers. "Yeah that's what I am talking about" said Nina with her hands in the air.

Chapter Sixteen

The DJ had played an old school song: Kool and the Gang "Cherish," that started up the party. As the song played, some people began to head to the dance floor.

"Oh, thanks again for bringing me Nina, I don't know what I would have done if I would had stayed home. I'll probably be bored out of mind," said Lyla.

"Girl you are welcome. You had to come out," responded Nina. Around this time, the DJ had changed the song into something mellow. The lights were dimmed and the mood of the air changed. In the mist of the crowd, a guy starred at Lyla all night. He stood in the shadows, waiting for the right time to approach her. He left his friend Darryl behind.

She was joking around and laughing with Nina, when the guy came over to talk to her. He must have been a sneaky puss because he came up from behind. As he approached Lyla, Nina watched from a distance as he slowly paced Lyla's way.

"Hello. I couldn't help but to notice you across the room looking so beautiful. Are you here with anyone?" asked the guy.

"Yes, but she has someone, maybe I could hang out with you," said Lyla flirting.

"That would be nice, I'm Benjamin," he said reaching for her hand. "Nice to meet you Benjamin, my name is Lyla Star. As Lyla slowly grabbed Benjamin's hand she felt the warmth of his touch, slowly tingling up her spine. Benjamin was very attractive. He wore this cologne that swallowed her completely.

After the Valentine's party, Benjamin and Lyla decided to grab a bite to eat somewhere. They became more acquainted.

"So, tell me more about you," said Benjamin as they walked into the cool night.

"Well, what would like to know first?" responded Lyla.

"Anything, it doesn't matter. Whatever you want to talk about," responded Benjamin. They walked to the nearest park and sat down on the swings.

"Well, my favorite colors are blue and red. My favorite food is Italian. I am very outspoken, if you haven't noticed already and I like to paint, sing, and dance. My father is a pastor at Pure of Heart Missionary Baptist Church and I am a born again Christian, which is my number one priority. What about you?" asked Lyla smiling like she just witnessed to the guy.

"Well, I think that I am a Christian. I mean I go to church sometimes." said Benjamin. His favorite colors were black and red. His favorite food was spaghetti, or anything with pasta noodles.

Chapter Seventeen

Still swinging back and forth, Lyla was curious to know why Benjamin showed up alone. He was definitely cute to be single. "So how did you hear about this party?" asked Lyla.

"I was invited by a friend, but honestly I was looking for someone that I had met online." replied Benjamin.

"Really, well does this somebody have a name? Maybe I could help you find this special lady." said Lyla.

"Yeah, her name is Ms. Sparkle, but she spells it like 'Mizz Sparkl3 which I think is quite sexy." replied Benjamin.

"Really, my friend is the one who pick it out for me. You really like it?" asked Lyla.

"Yeah, so you are Mizz Sparkl3? Wow! You are beautiful." said Benjamin.

"Well thank you very much. You wouldn't happen to be Chocolate Thunder by chance would you?" asked Lyla.

"Yes, I am Chocolate Thunder." said Benjamin.

"Well nice to meet you Chocolate Thunder," said Lyla exceeding her hand out to shake his again. Still warm as before, they both headed back to the party. When they got closer to the door, Benjamin grabbed Lyla by the hand and asked for a goodnight kiss before departing.

"Chocolate...wait! You don't know me yet, we barely know each other." said Lyla as she pushed him away.

"Then can I have your number?" asked Benjamin. He was very persistent. He didn't give up that easy.

"Oh, all right." Her number was...

"There you guys are. We've been looking for you guys for the longest time," said Nina and Darryl, Benjamin's friend.

"We were only talking, getting to know each other." said Benjamin. "You two could go back inside we will be there in a minute." Turning back to Lyla, he picked up from where they had left off. "Now where were we? Ah yeah. I was about to get your number."

"May I get your number first? I wouldn't feel comfortable giving out my number first," she asked.

Benjamin gave Lyla his number: (347) 225-3006. He asked for hers and she gave it to him. Both said goodnight to one another and went their separate ways.

Lyla was happy to have gone to the Valentine's party. Who would have known she'd meet her online guy. She had a feeling that something exciting would happen, well at least Nina did. He was gorgeous. Lyla knew that Benjamin had been checking her out, that's why he didn't want her to leave. She thought that she had handle the conversation pretty well, if not she was sure that Nina would had gave her some advice.

"So who was that cutie that you met tonight? He is very handsome." asked Nina.

"His name is Benjamin. His favorite food is spaghetti, his favorite colors are black and red..." responded Lyla without catching her breath.

"Wow! You are good. Normally it takes me a while to remember two or three things about a guy, but you remembered the important stuff." said Nina.

"Well, my father has always taught me to ask plenty of questions. That's how you can both learn and know if a guy is lying to you. If a man is lying, he would have to tell another lie to cover up the first lie." said Lyla.

"Have you been reading those "*Getting to know your new Man*" magazines again? Girl, how many times I have to tell you that those magazines don't work. That's how the illustrators get their viewers." said Nina. Normally, Nina would be right, but Lyla's father didn't raise any fool. In order to find out about anything, one had to ask questions.

Chapter Eighteen

As Lyla drifted off into a deep sleep, she dreamt about that handsome man, Chocolate Thunder. *Stranded on a remote island, Lyla shuddered as the waves rise toward her. "Who will save her now?" thought the abandon mistress.*

"I will, my lady." A man's voice came from the shadows.

"Who are you and where have you come from?" asked the woman.

"I have come from a beautiful place looking for a beautiful woman. I have heard your cries and have come to rescue you," said the man approaching the woman. Finally, her mate has come. As the man came closer, his face was revealed. It was Chocolate Thunder. He was shirtless. The sweat that appeared on his chest was tempting her to rub him down.

"Oh baby, come to mama," said the woman reaching out for him...

"Lyla what are you doing?" asked Nina. Lyla woke up with drenched blankets. "Were you having a fantasy?"

"I think I was. Can you tell me what happened? I don't remember." said Lyla.

"You had your arms stretched like you was trying to hug someone and chanting the words: *Oh baby, come to mama.* You were chanting that over and over again." said Nina. Was it about a fine man?"

"Girl, yes and yes. I had a dream about Benjamin. He was shirtless ripping with muscles...I could have sworn it was real." said Lyla. Slowly, Lyla was changing into someone that she hardly knew. She would have never lusted after a man. After dropping off Lyla at her house, Nina went to the store to get some groceries. Lyla opened the door to her two-bedroom condo. The condo was huge.

She had wooden hard floors, a modern couch with cream cushions and a matching love seat. She had a beautiful fire place. She had a 32 inch television that hung above the fireplace. In one bedroom, Lyla had a full size bed with cream sheets and linen with a dark and light green comforter. The pillows were color coordinated over the comforter. Lyla had a closet full of clothes and shoes.

In the other bedroom, Lyla had a black wooden desk with a matching black chair. On her desk were many pictures of her pet dogs, Charlie and Miley. Lyla's dogs were Havanese dogs. One dog, who was named Miley had a white straight coating and Charlie, was black with wavy thick coating. Both dogs were about ten pounds each and between the heights of eight point five to nine point five inches.

Lyla had several occupational careers. During the weekdays, she would work in her father's Industrial Stock Company on Mondays, Wednesdays, and Fridays mornings. She also volunteered at an Elementary school. Lyla was a devoted missionary for the Lord. She would be the inspirational speaker for several occasions. During Sunday mornings, Lyla had taught and work with the youths.

She was the coordinator of the Youth Department at her father's church Pure of Heart. In her living room, stood a beautiful black classic grand piano that was designed in such high-quality. The piano was about five to eight inches in length and forty-five point five feet in height. Outside her condo was a two car garage driveway that displayed her two nice cars. The first car was a black BMW convertible with cream leather seats and four doors. The second car was a white Porsche with brown leather interior.

"Hey Charlie and Miley did you miss mommy?" Lyla asked her dogs as she walked in the house. Charlie barked and jumped in the air frantically, while Miley rubbed Lyla's leg. "Aw, mommy misses you too. Let's go to the kitchen to get something to eat." As Lyla walked into the kitchen Charlie and Miley follow behind wagging their tails from side to side.

Chapter Nineteen

Later on that evening, Lyla cooked some fried fish and spaghetti with a side of green beans and biscuits. The food was delicious. As a beverage, Lyla drank some red wine which was acceptable to drink, since Jesus made some at a banquet; while soft music played in the background and Lyla sat close to the fireplace. *Ah, peace at last.* "Oh, how it feels good to be at home with my two babies," said Lyla rubbing Miley's with her right hand.

The warmth of the fire place lingered throughout the house. The atmosphere was very comforting. "Mommy is getting tired now, let's get ready for bed." As Lyla stood up to stretch her phone rang. "Hello?" said Lyla.

"Hey Lyla, It's Nina. How was your day?" asked Nina.

"My day was good, how was your day?" asked Lyla.

"Wonderful. Did you get a chance to talk to that cutie of yours?" asked Nina.

"No. I haven't called him yet." said Lyla.

"So? What's taking you so long? How come you haven't called him?" asked Nina. "You're wasting time."

"Ok, Nina. I'll call him jeez. Let me just relax for a little bit," said Lyla. Although, Lyla had found someone to talk to and could be with if she chose, she wasn't in desperation of having a man in her life. She strongly believed in waiting until it was the right time.

"Alright, don't let me down. Call him and then call me back when you two are done." said Nina.

"Ok, bye Nina," said Lyla quickly hanging up the phone. She finished the rest of the wine, before calling Benjamin. She checked the clock on the kitchen wall. It was 10:45pm. Oh my, she didn't know how late it was. Maybe she should call him in the morning when it was day. No, now would be better. Plus Nina would be upset if she waited until tomorrow. So she decided to call him tonight. Lyla hope it was not too late to call.

Lyla picked up the phone to dial Benjamin's number. She searched through her contacts and found his number. The number was 347-225-3006. Lyla dialed Benjamin's number. The phone rang twice, on the third ring she answered and heard a male's voice. "Hello?" asked the male's voice.

"Hello. May I speak to Benjamin?" asked Lyla.

"This is he. May I ask whose calling?" said Benjamin.

"This is Lyla. I met you at the Valentine's Day party." said Lyla.

"Oh, I remember you. You are the girl that didn't want to give me a kiss. Surprised that I still remember that minor event?" said Benjamin.

"Uh...yes. I thought that you had forgotten about that." said Lyla.

"No, I couldn't forget about the most beautiful girl I've ever saw. You are very pretty." said Benjamin.

"Well thank you very much. I was surprised when you answered. I thought that you would have been asleep by now or at work." Benjamin laughed.

"No, I normally work from Monday thru Thursday. Today I am off just thinking about you," said Benjamin.

"Oh really, where do you work at?" asked Lyla.

"I work as a bartender and you?" Before responding, Lyla thought about what he said. Benjamin worked as a bartender, so that meant either a club or bar. Hmmm…"I work as a stock assistant at my father's company. I've been working there for about two year's now." said Lyla.

"So when will I ever see you again?" asked Benjamin. Lyla didn't want to sound smart when she replied, but the words just sounded that way.

"Didn't you see me Thursday night?" said Lyla.

"Yeah, but I want to see you again. How's your Saturday looking? Can I see you tomorrow?" asked Benjamin.

"Maybe, if I do not have anything to do" She checked her schedule. So far she didn't have anything major to do. Lyla was happy. Finally, she was admired by a real physical man that had a great interest in her. Truly, the Lord had answered her prayers. Lyla wondered how she could ever thank Him for the blessing. Benjamin had his own: job, place, and car. He was definitely independent. Lyla adored the attention. Benjamin wanted to see her again.

"If we do go out, may I pick you up?" asked Benjamin. Lyla became a little hesitate. She really liked him, but felt a little nervous when she was alone with a man. Lyla guessed that the cause came from her father's sheltering. Reverend Johnson had always been protective of his daughter. "Lyla, are you still there?" asked Benjamin sighing at Lyla's silence.

"Uh…hey. Sorry. Benjamin I can just meet you. I'll drive my own car." said Lyla.

"You don't trust me? I would really like to pick you up. Leave your car at home and ride with me," said Benjamin.

"Ben, I am coming with you. We are just in separate cars. Have you ever been to V's Italian restaurant?" asked Lyla.

"No! How come you won't let me pick you up? I'm trying to be a gentleman here." said Benjamin.

"Just meet me at the restaurant around 6:30pm, please and have a good night." said Lyla as she hung up the phone.

Chapter Twenty

When Lyla got off the phone with Benjamin, she was very disturbed. He sounded very persuasive over the phone and when she refused to give in to his requests, he got an attitude. Lyla wondered what his problem was. Lyla wasn't obligated to do anything she didn't want to. She called Nina and told her what happened.

"So tell me what happened again? You called Benjamin last night and he had invited you to dinner at a restaurant. And now you think that he is a jerk?" said Nina. "Girl, what is wrong with you?"

"Yes, I mean no. I did call him last night, but I don't think that he is a jerk. I just think that he is so weird," said Lyla. It was Saturday afternoon, when Lyla called Nina.

"Weird? No, Lyla you are crazy. The guy likes you. What's so weird about that?" said Nina.

"I don't know. I just feel a little funny about this. Maybe I am just worried," said Lyla.

"Well, don't be. Benjamin seems like a nice guy. You should give him a chance," said Nina.

"Alright, I'll give him a chance. What's the worst thing that could happen?" said Lyla. "I'll call you after the dinner."

"Ok, have fun!!" said Nina.

Lyla looked at the clock on the kitchen wall. It was a quarter 'til five. Lyla ran to her room to get dressed. She had taken a bath earlier around 5:30pm before talking to Nina. Her dress was laying on the bed. The dress was beautiful. The color of the dress was emerald green and the strap went around Lyla's neck revealing her caramel skin. Lyla looked sexy. She curled her hair and pinned it with an emerald hair pin. She mustered to get loose long curls to fall on the side. Lyla puts on her earrings and eye shadow.

She added some red lipstick. *You are simply gorgeous!* Lyla sat on her bed to put on her heels, when Benjamin text her:

"Hey beautiful are you ready for dinner?" texted Benjamin

"Yeah, are you?" texted Lyla

"Just about, I hope you dress to impress, because I sure did. I look bad in my suit." texted Benjamin

"Me too, I look so fine." texted Lyla

"I bet you do…so where is the restaurant located?" texted Benjamin

"The restaurant is off of 53rd street by Michael's." texted Lyla

"Oh, I know where it is at. Are you going to be there at 6:30pm?" texted Benjamin

"I'll probably get there around 6:30pm." texted Lyla

"Ok, then text or call me when you get there. I don't stay that far from the restaurant, so it will only take me five to ten minutes." texted Benjamin.

"Ok, see you then." texted Lyla

Lyla looked in the mirror to straighten her dress. She slightly moved a strand of her bangs and turned to look at Charlie and Miley. "Ok, how do I look?" Lyla asked Charlie and Miley. Charlie barked and Miley hopped on her feet. I'll take that as approved. Lyla patted her dogs on their heads. "Aw, I have such adorable pets. Mommy loves you, yes she does," she made cute faces.

Lyla went to the kitchen to put some Beneful in the dog bowls and some fresh water before grabbing her car keys and leaving out the door. Lyla decided to drive her white Porsche. She texted Benjamin:

"Hey I'm heading there now, so I'll see you soon."

She put on her seat belt and put the keys in the ignition. She turned on the radio and drove with some mellow music. When Lyla got to the restaurant, she can't believe her eyes. Benjamin wore this clean black suit looking sharp. Benjamin looked so handsome. "Wow! You look great!" said Lyla.

"Me? You're the one that looks good with your emerald green dress," said Benjamin.

"You know, I don't think the restaurant is ready for us. We look like two celebrities that have just come out of Hollywood," said Lyla.

"I know what you mean, well what can we say? We got it going on," said Benjamin.

Chapter Twenty-One

"May I take your hand, my queen?" asked Benjamin.

"Yes you may," responded Lyla. As Benjamin grabbed Lyla's hand, they walked into the restaurant as a couple. The restaurant had soft lights inside with burgundy curtains. There were several couples and families that came out. The atmosphere was very warm and welcoming. Lyla and Benjamin had chosen a perfect night to go out. The temperature outside was nice as the moon glowed in the starless night.

A smile appeared on Benjamin's face, "where would you like to sit?" asked Benjamin.

"Somewhere close by the window," said Lyla.

"How about those windows over there by the wall?" asked Benjamin.

"Those windows are fine," said Lyla. "Have you ever eaten here before?"

"No. But I've heard that they serve really good food," said Benjamin.

"Someone have told me the same thing," said Lyla.

"Hello, welcome to V's. My name is Kellie and I would be your waitress this evening," said Kellie. *"Can I start you off with a beverage?"*

"No, not at the moment. But we both can have a glass of water." said Lyla.

"Alright. I will get those for you. Let me know when you are ready to order, said Kellie.

"Ok, thank you," said Benjamin.

"You are welcome." said Kellie.

Benjamin gently rubbed Lyla's hand. His hand felt warm and a scent of his cologne made Lyla blush. He was such a gentleman. "You look so beautiful tonight," said Benjamin.

"And you look handsome." said Lyla. They began to look at the menu.

"What do you have a craving for? asked Benjamin.

"I don't know, but I would like to try that Mozzarella cheese pasta that has the tomato brasil sauce and chopped grilled peppers," said Lyla.

"Ohh, that sounds good. But I think that I am going to try the grilled chicken that is smothered in mushroom with steam white rice," said Benjamin.

"Ohh, that sounds even better," said Lyla.

"So have you decided on a beverage yet?" asked Kellie as she approached the table. "Well, I was thinking about ordering one of your finiest wine," said Benjamin. "But wasn't for sure if that is what Lyla wants, so I am still undecided."

"Would that be something that you would like to get?" Kellie asked Lyla.

"Yes, that would be alright. Make sure that it is your finist," said Lyla.

"Oh, I sure will. Have you decided on your dinner?" asked Kellie.

"Yes, I would have the Mozzarella cheese pasta with the tomato basil sauce and grilled peppers," said Lyla.

"And I would have the grilled chicken that is smothered in mushroom with steam white rice," said Benjamin.

"Alright, sounds like you both had selected two delicious meals," said Kellie. "I shall return with both orders and the finist wine that is requested." Kellie took the menus and headed toward the back. Shortly, she returned with both orders on one huge platter and later with the wine. The time was coming to an end. So far, the night with Benjamin was going well. Surprisingly, Lyla had a good time and felt awful that she so quickly judge him without giving him a chance. The dinner was delicious and the wine was excellent.

"Thank you again for inviting me to dinner. I really had a nice time," said Lyla.

"You are welcome. I hope that we can do this again. I really like spending time with you." said Benjamin.

"Me too. You are such a gentleman. I would call you once I get home. Have a good night Benjamin," said Lyla. As she headed home, she couldn't help but to smile all night. Again, truly God had blessed her.

Chapter Twenty-Two

Awakening by the bright sun that appeared through the blinds, Lyla had never seen the sun shine so beautifully. She thought that she was in love. Cupid must had zap on the love bug within her. After spending most of her life single, Lyla had given up on trying to find a good man. But after last night, her whole perspective of not finding a good man had changed. Benjamin was so attractive and sweet. She truly believed that he was the man that God had prepared for her. She prayed: Please Lord let it be so.

"Good morning, beautiful. How are you feeling today?" texted Benjamin.

"I am doing well handsome. How are you feeling today?" texted Lyla.

"Um, I'm okay. I wish that you were here with me though." texted Benjamin.

"Oh really? How did you sleep last night?" texted Lyla.

"I slept okay. I really wish that you had stayed the night with me. I couldn't stop thinking about you." texted Benjamin.

Wow! Lyla couldn't believe what she was hearing. Did he just say what she thought he said? Benjamin wanted Lyla to spend the night with him. They had only known each other for two days. Lyla couldn't believe what she was hearing.

But could she blame him? Lyla was very attractive. She was healthy with her curvy figure. Her hair was so long and wavy. Lyla didn't have any children. She made decent money and led several group sessions for youths and battered women.

Lyla played a huge part in her community, while maintaining her self-image as a Pastor's daughter. She definitely knew that her appearance could entice any man to want her. Her father use to say that she was born with his good looks and her mother's long hair. Well wasn't she the blessed one. She had an adorable mother.

"Hey Lyla are you still there?" texted Benjamin.

"Yeah I'm still here." texted Lyla.

"Let me get myself dressed first than I'll give you a call when I am finished." texted Lyla.

"Alright. I'll talk to you later." texted Benjamin.

"Ok, call you when I'm done." texted Lyla. She was still in the bed. It was a quarter 'til twelve. Lyla rolled out of bed. The strap of her gown had fallen down showing a small peek of her bosom. She was sweaty from last night temperature. She needed to hop in the shower quickly. She looked through her drawer to find some under garments, when her door bell rang.

Who could this be? Lyla walked toward the door. Her dogs were on their mats asleep. "Who is it?" said Lyla.

"It's me Nina. Girl open up the door." said Nina.

"Hey girl. I was just about to call you. How are you today?" said Lyla.

"I am doing fine. So where is that sexy man of yours, upstairs perhaps?" asked Nina.

"No, he's at home." said Lyla.

"He didn't spend the night? How could you just send him home. Girl you couldn't be me. I would have had him all cuddled up under me." said Nina. "He is so fine."

"I know that he is attractive, Nina. But I hardly even know the man to sleep with him. How come everyone is talking about sex all the time," said Lyla.

"Girl, that is the only time that I have mentioned sex. Who else have been talking about it?" asked Nina.

"Benjamin!" He texted me earlier and said that he wished that I was there with him. He said that I should have spent the night with him," said Lyla.

"Wow! Are you serious? He said that to you? asked Nina.

"Yes, he did. Girl, let me take a shower than we can talk some more over a cup of coffee," said Lyla.

"Ok girl. Try to hurry up and get dress, so we can talk," said Nina.

Chapter Twenty-Three

Lyla found some under garments and went to her room to take a shower. She turned the knob for hot water and caressed her body with soap. After taking her shower, Lyla got dressed and headed back downstairs where Nina was at. She wore a white blouse with a navy blue blazer, a khaki skirt, and light tan heels. She pinned her hair into a bun and gently sprayed a mist of Forever Elizabeth perfume.

"Well are you very pretty. I like those shoes and that khaki skirt," said Nina.

"Thanks girl. You know I have never wore this skirt before and it fits perfectly on me," said Lyla. "I knew that walking would do me some good."

"Maybe, but you do look very nice," said Nina.

"Again, thank you. Would you like a cup of coffee?" asked Lyla.

"No. Some hot tea would be fine for me. So what else happened?" asked Nina.

"Dinner went well. We went to that V's Italian Restaurant on 53rd street by Michael's and had a great time. I had wore my emerald green dress with the strap going around my neck showing my back and Benjamin had wore his clean black suit with his black gator shoes. My hair was curled and pinned to the side and his fade was lined up," said Lyla.

"Was you two looking sharp?" asked Nina.

"You know it. We walked in that restaurant like we owned the place. All eyes was on us," said Lyla. "We found a table by the window and ordered our meals. Benjamin had requested a bottle of wine and the fire was lit," said Lyla.

"Aww..doesn't that sound romantic?" said Nina.

"It was. The scenery was amazing," said Lyla.

"I bet it was. Well girl I'm about to go home and sleep for a little while," said Nina. "I'm glad you had fun. Do you think that Benjamin have any brothers?"

"I don't think so. I would have to ask him the next time I see him," said Lyla.

"Ok. Girl let me know if Benjamin has any so we could date. I want to have a chocolate brother on my arm as well," said Nina. " Should I try the Black Single chatline again?"

"Maybe, if you are desperate. But I thought that you were already dating someone?" asked Lyla.

"I was, but I got bored with him and left. Now I am single again, " said Nina with excitement. "I wonder who would be the next brother that's going to ride this train."

"Nina, slow down. You shouldn't be so quick in finding another man. When it is the right time a good man will come along," said Lyla.

"That's easy for you to say, Lyla. You already have a good man. You are not the single and lonely one." said Nina.

"I was before, but I waited on God. Now I have a good man," said Lyla. "All I am saying is wait on God and He will provide."

"I hope so, because my patience is running thin," said Nina.

"It will happen. Just wait and see," said Lyla.

Later on that evening, Lyla called Benjamin to see how he was. She took a hot bath with ton of bubbles and vanilla scent candles that were scattered all over the bathroom. Lyla rubbed her body down with brown sugar lotion and put on her silky black robe. Her hair hung behind her back. Benjamin was happy to get her call. She knew this because she heard the excitement in his voice. "Hey handsome, are you still awake?" asked Lyla.

"Hey sugar. I'm still up. What are you doing?" asked Benjamin.

"Nothing, I'm just laying down. I would have called you earlier, but I was talking to my friend and lost track of the time," said Lyla.

"Oh it's okay. I kind of figure that you were busy. Do you have any plans for tomorrow?" asked Benjamin.

"No. Just church in the morning. Would you like to hang out afterwards? asked Lyla.

"We can if you are free. What will you like to do?" asked Benjamin.

"Anything. I just want to spend time with you. We can go to the movies or out to eat. Whatever you want to do, "said Lyla.

"Really? Could I spend the night if I wanted too?"asked Benjamin. "If I am not mistaken, you did say anything."

"Only activity wise." said Lyla. "I don't want us to move fast in our friendship. I would have to think about it." Then again, what was there to think about. Benjamin and her were not married, why should she even be thinking about sensual actions. Lord help Lyla.

"Well, think about it and let a brotha know," said Benjamin. "I am ready to be your man. Are you ready to be my woman?"

"Benjamin I think that you are moving a little too fast. Are you ready to do all of that?" asked Lyla.

"Of course I am," said Benjamin. "If I wasn't, I wouldn't have asked you."

Again, Benjamin manage to ask if he could spend the night over Lyla's house. She thought that she had made her self clear when she said No! Lyla needed help. She didn't know what to do. She didn't want to be rude, so she began to pray and asked God for help.

Chapter Twenty-Four

Lyla what does your heart say? Should she lay down or let down? If she chosed one, would the consequences be small or great? Was Benjamin and Lyla moving too fast or was this acceptable because this was what people do when they were seriously involved? Question after question circled in Lyla's mind. "Benjamin I'm sorry, but I have to go. It's getting very late and I am very tired." said Lyla. "Would it be alright if I called you tomorrow after church?"

"Yeah that's fine. Just call me when you have time," said Benjamin. "I hope you have some sweet dreams about me, because I know I'll have some of you."

"Of course I will handsome. Have a good night," said Lyla.

"You too, have a good night my queen," said Benjamin. His words sounded so sweet. Lyla hung up the phone and glanced at the clock on her night stand. The time was two-thirty A.M. Lyla stretched her legs and arms before fallen asleep. She had awaken minutes later to set her alarm and she said her prayers. Lyla got up around a quarter 'til eight. Her alarm clock went off. Lyla got out of the bed and headed toward the bathroom to wash her face and brush her teeth.

After brushing her teeth, Lyla went back into her room and said her prayers. Then she searched for her bra and panties in her drawer and took a shower. Lyla had set her church attire on the bed with her black stockings. Lyla's attire was a red flowery dress that buttoned all the way to the top. Her brown leather boots was lined up against the closet door. Lyla had clipped her hair and put on some make-up. She sprayed a mist of perfume and headed toward the kitchen.

Charlie and Miley jumped on Lyla, but missed touching her by only an inch. They had to go outside to take care of their business, so Lyla opened the patio door and let Charlie and Miley out. She cooked a quick breakfast. One scrabbled egg, two turkey patties and some toast. She looked in the refrigerador for some apple juice and found some orange juice. She poured a glass. After eating her breakfast, Lyla glanced at her watch.

The time was nine-thirty A.M. She opened the patio door to let Charlie and Miley back inside. Lyla wasn't sure if she would make it to Sunday School on time, so she decided to leave around ten-thirty for the morning service that started at eleven. Lyla placed her dirty dishes in the sink and washed them. After washing the dishes, she hung them on the dish rack. Lyla looked in the refrigerador to see if she had anymore apples.

She only had two apples left, grabbing one she closed the refrigerador door. The apple was cold and fresh, just like she liked it. She glanced at the watch again. It was ten-ten. She decided to leave a little early and put two cups of Beneful and some fresh water in Charlie and Miley's bowls. Finishing her apple, Lyla grabbed her Holy Bible and went outside. She started up the car and drove to church.

The church was located on 35th and Cleveland. The church was called Pure of Heart Baptist. The name had come from the ideal image of Christianity. The ideal change; changing from the mind to the heart. Lyla was so excited about going to church. She got excited when she thought about Jesus. Lyla pulled up in the driveway. Many of the members were just arriving. "Good morning, Sis. Mary. How are you today?" asked Lyla shaking Mary's hand in a warm gesture.

"I'm doing fine. How are you Lyla?" asked Mary.

"Oh, I'm happy to be here," said Lyla.

Lyla walked into the church with a smile on her face. Sunday mornings always seem to be a warm and beautiful day. The whole atmosphere seem to be at peace. While entering the church, the choir sung Lyla's favorite song: "Oh, Lord How Excellent." She loved that song. The choir wore their purple robes, looking all sharp and clean. Swaying from side to side, Lyla leaped on her feet and clapped her hands. *Come on in Holy Spirit. You are welcome in this place called HEART,* said Lyla lifting up her hands.

So far the church service was going well, but Lyla was ready to hear the powerful word from her father, Pastor Johnson. She wondered what today's lesson would be. After the choir sang their last song, Lyla's father came to the pulpit. "Good morning everyone and welcome to Pure of Heart Baptist Church. If you are a member we are glad that you are here and if your a visitor welcome again. Before I begin the lesson, I would like to start off with a prayer," said Rev. Johnson:

Heavenly Father we acknowledge your presence on this day. Lord, we thank you for your mercy and your grace. Lord, we ask that you would open up our hearts to receive your Word and apply the lesson to our everyday lives. Lord let your presence be seen and your message come forth. All these things I ask in Jesus name Amen.

The scripture came from Genesis 29:18-20 and the Bible reads: "*As Jacob traveled to the east, he came across some family members that were giving water to the flocks of sheep. The members were the daughters of Laban, the brother of Jacob's* mother. When Laban heard about his sister's son being in town, Laban met, embraced and kissed him. Then he invited Jacob into his house. Laban had provide space and ask him what wages should he gain if Jacob was to work for him. When Jacob seen how beautiful Rachel was, he was willing to work seven years for the hand of Rachel in marriage. Since Jacob was so deeply in love with Rachel, the years to him were only a few days."

When Jacob saw the winning prize of having Rachel as his wife, he was willing to do anything for her father to have her. Jacob worked for seven years to get Rachel. SEVEN YEARS! Who do you know would work for seven years to marry a woman? Or better yet someone who would work period? The love that Jacob had for Rachel was far greater than any labor. Real love preserveres. Before I take my seat, I want to leave everyone with this thought, how far are you willing to go to get your prize? Jesus our Lord and our Savior was willing to go all the way to demonstrate his love for us.

Lyla how far are you willing to go? The message was powerful. The Word had come from God to me, thought Lyla. He was asking her if the relationship between Benjamin and her was worth hard labor? Would Benjamin be willing to work for Lyla's heart? Would she be willing to work for his? Of course she would, nothing could change the way Lyla felt about Benjamin. They were inseparable, well that was what she thought until she found out about Benjamin's secrets.

Chapter Twenty-Five

Ever since there first date, Lyla and Benjamin had been hanging out everyday. They had schedule several lunch dates together and Benjamin had even offer to cook dinner every night for the both of them. One night, Benjamin made chicken Alfredo with some wheat french bread being the bowl, so the dinner turned out to be very extraordinary. For the dessert, they made sundaes with French Vanilla ice cream, chocolate syrup and crushed nuts.

On Tuesday afternoon, they went to the movies, than afterwards went to the mall. Lyla was digging her new boyfriend and her boo was digging her to. Everyday they were together. When Benjamin asked her the question of moving in together, the relationship between them would be official. Is this something you want to do? asked Lyla.

"Yes, I think that it would be an excellent idea, if we are planning to be together," said Benjamin.

"Oh I don't know, Benjamin. I still think that we are moving too fast," said Lyla. Whenever Lyla was in tight situations like one of these, the voice of her father would pop up in the back of her mind: *When you find a nice boyfriend, he should be loyal and patient with you. He should never pressure you or force you to do something that you are not ready for. Listen to the Holy Spirit. The Spirit will never steer you wrong.*

"So what do you want to do Lyla? Can we move in together? asked Benjamin.

"Maybe we could try, Benjamin do you love me?" asked Lyla. The words just flew out her mouth without her giving much thought about them. She wasn't expecting those words so soon.

"Of course I do. I really do care about you," said Benjamin. "And I think you should be my dime piece. I want you to be my woman."

"And I want you to be my man," said Lyla. Again, he spoke his slang that made Lyla melted. They had been dating for about four months now and their relationship was growing stronger and stronger. Sometime, Lyla wondered if anything bad could ever happen to them. They seem like the perfect couple until the fifth month rolled in, changing the vibe from peace to choas. Their relationship went from wonderful to horrible when they decided to move in together.

Lyla was so busy with her church meetings that she didn't see how lonely Benjamin got at times. Benjamin would come home so drunk and wasted that he had forgotten how to treat Lyla. Oh my, she didn't know how busy her calendar would be for this month. On Monday afternoon, Lyla signed up to direct the youth choir and on Tuesday morning, she had breakfast with her father, the senior Pastor. On Wednesday evening, Lyla was ask to teach the Bible Study lesson for the adult class.

On Thursday afternoon, Lyla had to teach her piano class how to play this: "This Little Light of Mine" and "Jesus Loves Me." On Friday night, Lyla had to host one of her teen's group session and cook a dinner for mother Bernice's nephew. On Saturday evening, she was supposed to have dinner with Benjamin, but had to cancel their reservation when she was told to join the women of the church for powerful prayer. On

Sunday morning, Lyla had to teach a Sunday school class, so she made sure to study the lesson before-hand.

Lyla was afraid to look at her next week schedule.

"You're probably to busy next week and the week after that to hang out with me," said Benjamin. "Sometimes I think that serving the Lord is way important than being with me."

"Well yes, I mean no. I mean…I love you." She tried to think of quick comforting words. "You knew what you were getting yourself into when you started dating me. I told you how serving God is my number one priority. I am sorry that I haven't been spending time with you, but what did you expect? Me to drop everything and end my busy schedule for you?" asked Lyla.

"Yes. Something has to give. I thought that you cared about me?" asked Benjamin.

"I do care about you Benjamin, but I have to do what makes me happy. I like helping at the church and you know this," said Lyla.

"Man, whatever. If you don't change your schedule and spend more time with me you are going to regret the consequences," said Benjamin.

"Are you kidding me?" Benjamin was upset because she liked to go to church and serve God. Lyla couldn't help that, but she did see his point. She needed to spend more time with him, but all he wanted to do was stay in-doors and cuddle all the time. There was a bigger world out there and she felt that she shouldn't be coop up inside all the time. Maybe if he came along with Lyla and participated in at least one event, he wouldn't had felt so lonely. But then again, only God knows. *Live in Harmony*..Romans 12:16. Lyla was trying too, but this guy was really working her nerves.

Alright Lord, she decided to change her schedule a little, so that she could spend more time with Benjamin. She just hope that he didn't do anything foolish.

Looking at her schedules, Lyla didn't know where to begin. Should she reschedule all her church meetings or all of her piano lessons? Maybe if she shuffled both meetings, she would have had a more complex plannar. Perhaps, she should try to see if that would work first before changing anything else. She began with the most current events, than work through the following, but she had already set several permanant dates and times for many events that it would seem impossible to reschedule or change anything. Lyla knew that she had to think fast before Benjamin began to complain about something else.

Should she try recalling everyone first than rescheduling? Maybe, but would that even work? "Benjamin, where are you sweetie?" asked Lyla. He was in the living room sitting on the couch. Charlie and Miley were agitating him, so he sent them away. They barked when he sent them to the patio.

"I am in here," said Benjamin. "So what are you going to do?"

"I have decided to try rescheduling some of my meetings, so that I can spend some more time with you," said Lyla.

"Alright, that sounds better. Now what are you going to do with the dogs?" asked Benjamin.

"Nothing, my dogs are not going anywhere. Do you have a problem with them? asked Lyla.

"Yes I do. I don't like them. I think that you should give them away," said Benjamin.

"What? Are you crazy? I love my puppies," said Lyla. "How come you are making things so difficult? My dogs are not leaving and that's that." In the back of her mind, Lyla was tempted to be rude, but didn't because that could had resulted in a fight or even worse him leaving her. "Maybe we should try compromising first."

"Compromising? What needs to be compromised? The dogs are leaving," said Benjamin. Lyla grabbed her coat and left the house. She just needed to clear her head. Lyla drove her BMW. Lord please help her relationship with Benjamin. She really would had like for them to compromise and got alone. Lyla drove to the park.

She had just left church and now she felt the need of returning back to get some more anointing. How come her relationship was so difficult? The weather was warm, when the sunset appeared. Lyla removed her coat. She still had on her red flowery dress and shoes that she wore for church that morning. Benjamin didn't go to church. He stayed at home with the supposedly horrible dogs.

At the park, a slight wind pushed the swings as fallen leaves skipped along the covered aspalt. The slide rails were cold as droplets of water and fell in a round puddle that sat at the end of the slide. When Lyla saw a glimpse of the moon, she was reminded of how late it was getting. She looked at her watch. The time was a quarter 'til eleven. She knew that she should be heading back now.

Lyla walked back to her car and sat back in the seat. She hoped that Benjamin had calmed down some, she would have hated to come home to an angry boyfriend. But when she drove up in the driveway, she had soon realized how she would be the person that became angry.

Chapter Twenty-Six

When Lyla approached the house, she heard loud music blasting inside and saw half-naked women running in and out the house. What the hell..excuse me Jesus..was going on here, thought Lyla. "BENJAMIN!!" yelled Lyla as she walked inside. "BENJAMIN!!" she yelled again.

"Hey, why all the yelling? We didn't do anything wrong," said a man heading toward the dining room. Lyla followed the man into the dinning room and saw Benjamin sitting on the couch with another woman on his lap. The woman looked familiar. "Benjamin did you here me calling you? asked Lyla.

"What? Oh, hey Lyla. When did you get home?" asked Benjamin.

"Just now. Benjamin, are you drunk? asked Lyla.

"No, I feel good," said Benjamin. "Did not James Brown say that? I feel good." He leaned forward to whisper something in the woman's ear and she turned her head, Nina! Nina giggled and stood up to walk away. As she left, Benjamin's slapped her on the butt. "Make it jiggle baby," said Benjamin. "Lyla come sit on big daddy's lap." No! Lyla became furious.

"No, Benjamin you're drunk," said Lyla.

"No I'm not. I am perfectly fine. Would you please give me a hug or at least sit by me? said Benjamin.

"No, why was Nina sitting on your lap?" asked Lyla. Benjamin shrugged his shoulders," I don't know, she slipped and fell on my lap."

"Oh really. Do you think that I'm dumb? asked Lyla. "I leave for a couple of hours and you invite all these people to my house?"

"Correction, don't you mean *our* house. They're only friends," said Benjamin. "When you left earlier, I was lonely. So I called a few people and they invited their friends. Next thing I knew, the house was packed with people."

"Oh how nice," Lyla said sarcastically. "You didn't think to call me and let me know that you were inviting Nina over? I would have dressed up for the occassion."

"No you wouldn't. You would have gave me a lecture or something. But enough about me, where have you been all this time? asked Benjamin.

"I went to the park to clear my head. I was so frustrated and upset about our argument, that I needed to escape," said Lyla. "I didn't mean to leave you alone, I should have called you."

"Yeah, you should have. You had me worrying about you," said Benjamin. Still that didn't change the fact that he was wrong. Benjamin knew better. "I missed my boo."

"Yeah right? You are here getting your groove on," said Lyla. Again, she asked Benjamin about Nina sitting on his lap. "Why was Nina sitting on your lap?" Benjamin's face expression changed when Lyla asked the question. "Why was Nina on your lap?" she asked again.

"What? I told you that she slipped down," said Benjamin. "So don't ask me anymore." She wondered how much more can she put up with this foolishness.

"Oh, it's like that Benjamin? That's cool. I got something for you," said Lyla. He would get his tonight, thought Lyla and continued to smile in his face.

"Hey bro, we were looking for you. Where have you been hiding?" Two guys were coming out of the kitchen to approach Benjamin. "Who is this foxy mama? Can I have your name and number?" asked the taller guy from the two.

"What's up Benny and Skip. I didn't know you guys were here. What's happening?" said Benjamin.

"Nothing really. Just trying to find some skin I can rub. Who's this pretty girl by you?" the taller guy asked.

"Oh, this beautiful lady is my girl. Fellas meet Lyla and Lyla meet the fellas, Darryl and Jarod Miller, also known as Benny and Skip." said Benjamin. Darryl was the taller guy. He had braids with polished white beads at the end of them. He wore some dark shades with a mouth of aluminum sliver on his teeth, which was not appealing to Lyla. His brother, Jarod was shorter and chubby. He had an afro and wore these rectangular glasses.

The brothers went by the name Benny and Skip. Benny was Darryl's nickname and Skip was Jarod's nickname. "Nice to meet you fellas. I've heard so little about you," said Lyla, she was only being honest. She was still upset about Benjamin's encounter with Nina and the surprised party.

"Bro, you've been keeping her to yourself? You should have told us about this cutie" said Darryl. They thought that she was fine.

"Thank you. And you are charming yourself," said Lyla.

"Girl, you don't have to tell me. I know I look good," said Darryl. Already, she could tell that he was conceited.

Chapter Twenty-Seven

"Should I pour you a drink? asked Benjamin. "We got plenty in the kitchen."

"No. I am not thirsty." said Lyla. She was still trying to figure out why Nina was on his lap. "Well, maybe some water. She rubbed her throat. Suddenly, she was in need for a drink.

"Water? You want some water? That's not a drink. Come follow me in the kitchen. I have patron, Vodka, Moscato wine in any flavor, gin…whatever you want," said Benjamin. "You know that I am the local bartender around here."

"Of course you are," said Lyla, thinking to herself *why boast about such drunkeness.* "But you know how I feel about alcohol, plus I'm too tired to drink anything else other than water." said Lyla.

"Than more for us," said Darryl. "It was really nice meeting you, Lyla. Maybe I could be your boyfriend number two."

"I don't think so, you aight but you ain't my type," said Lyla. "You didn't know that I could talk that slang did you? I haven't always been proper."

"Really? You keep talking like that and and…what's going to happen to her Benny," asked Jarod.

"Oh, you speak? You have a lovely voice," said Lyla. She was use of hearing Benny's voice, but haven't heard Skip say anything at all. Now he spoke for a change.

"Well thank you you, Lyla," said Jarod. Lyla noticed how Jarod stuttered when he spoke.

"She will find out," said Benny. Lyla tried not to reveal her disputes with Benjamin before his friends that would be very rude of her, so she waited for another time to speak her mind.

"I'm about to go to bed," said Lyla. She kissed him on his cheeks, then walk toward the bedroom. As Lyla walked, she noticed a pair of eyes watching her. Benny starred at Lyla as she walked away. He was very drunk and Lyla looked good to him. He had to get her. Benny was so caught in the moment that he didn't hear Benjamin call him.

"Benny, are you alright? Did you make the drop earlier?" asked Benjamin. "I have a few clients that is in need of a high."

"Yeah, I'm straight. And the drop has already been made," said Benny. "Ah man, I'm about to head back to the crib. Call me later when you have time."

"Alright. You call me when you get home so that I know you've made it," said Benjamin.

"Ok, talk to you later," said Darryl. Benjamin followed Lyla upstairs. "You know Lyla that kiss you gave me earlier lit up my flame," said Benjamin.

"Oh really? Are you going to explode? asked Lyla.

"Maybe. Let me kick everyone out first than I'll be right up," said Benjamin.

"Don't talk like that. Those people are your friends," said Lyla. "Plus, I'm not in the mood to cuddle tonight." She was still upset about Benjamin's actions that were done earlier.

"What? You are not in the mood? That's crazy talk Lyla. Let me get rid of these folks," said Benjamin. Lyla was serious about what she said. She and Benjamin had been dating for about seven months and she still hadn't received a ring from him. She couldn't take this anymore. If he really loved her, how come he couldn't buy her a ring? She thought to herself. She was beginning to sound like her fahter. Her patience became thin. She was tired of being Benjamin's dime piece, she wanted to be in his heart.

Meanwhile, Benjamin headed back to the living room to get rid of his guests. "Hey everybody! The party has been shut down and moved somewhere else. Come back next week, when there is more food and booze," said Benjamin. Aw...the crowd moaned, but cheered up quickly when he said next week more booze. The crowd gathered their things and left the condo. Benjamin locked the door and marched to the bedroom where Lyla laid.

Lyla pretended to be asleep. Her eyes were closed and the blanket was wrapped around her. "Lyla are you asleep?" asked Benjamin. "I hope not because I need you badly tonight." Benjamin had quite a few drinks, which left him with a strong urge. Lyla's eyes remain closed. "Come on Lyla. Sweetie I need you. Would you please wake up for me," said Benjamin. He began to shake her gently, but that didn't work.

So he shook her again. "Lyla wake up, Lyla wake up. Wake up sweetie," said Benjamin. But she didn't move. He began to puff and let out a huge sign. "Lyla WAKE UP! I'm not playing with you. You need to get up NOW!" said Benjamin. He got angry with her. Lyla couldn't take it anymore. She opened her eyes and turned around. Benjamin starred at the ceiling, lying on his back. "Benjamin, you didn't see me sleeping here? What do you want?" asked Lyla.

She knew what he wanted, but she wasn't giving him anything. "Lyla, are you mad at me?" asked Benjamin. "Are you trying to tell me something?" Lately, Lyla has been holding out on Benjamin. Her gate has been locked and her door has been shut. She wondered if he would ever get it.

Chapter Twenty-Eight

"The time goes by so slow when you are at work. I can't wait to go home," said Lyla as she stared at the clock on the wall. The firm was in session and her father wanted to expand the bonds into threes.

"We need more stockholders...lawyers, judges... any one. When the business rises we rise," said Al Johnson. "Lyla what's your opinion?"

"Dad, I don't know. We could release more stock chambers for stockshares," said Lyla.

"True, but where would...Lyla's dad could go on and on about the firm, but she had enough. "Can anyone think of anything?" asked Al Johnson. The room grew silent. "Fine, the meeting was adjourned. We are dismissed."

Hallelujah! They all shouted. Everyone was happy, but Al Johnson was disappointed. "We still haven't thought of a plan," said Al Johnson.

"Oh we will, Father have faith. I know you are concerned about your company, but God's got your back. You shouldn't worry," said Lyla.

"You are right, that's why you are my baby. Come give your daddy some love," said Al Johnson. Lyla leaped in his arms. She felt like a child again. "Oh, I love you daddy," said Lyla.

"And I love you too Lyla," said Al Johnson.

Tonight was a full house. There were at least thirty children at the youth choir rehearsal. After Lyla left work, she went home to take a nap. Benjamin had Benny and Skip over last night, so she didn't get much sleep. When she woke up, it was five-thirty p.m. The choir rehearsal began at six-thirty. Lyla took a nice shower. She placed her clothes on the bed before taking her shower. Lyla decided to wear her blue Levi's and a white blouse. When she arrived at the church, she was very happy.

"Hello everyone!" Lyla said as she looked around the church. Eddie, the choir director had come early to open the door to the sanctuary.

"Hello Ms. Star!" said the children.

"Oh, they are so adorable," said Lyla to Eddie.

"Yes, they are. Are you ready to begin?" asked Eddie.

"Of course." said Lyla."What songs are we practicing tonight?"

"Well, I was thinking about singing some soft contemporary hymns for the Lord. You know jazz it up a little bit." said Eddie. "There's this one song I've been listening to a lot, the title of the song appears to be strange, but the message of the song is very sentimental."

"Oh really, what type of song is called that?" asked one of the children.

"A song that is going to lift up our Lord Jesus Christ," said Lyla. "Let's give it a try. What are the words to the song?" Eddie walked toward the piano and played the song. He began to sing it.

"Wow! How beautiful." said Lyla. "I think the song is excellent."

"I need all sopranos in front, the contrattos in center, and the tenors in back please. Lyla did you bring your acoustic guitar?" asked Eddie.

"No. I didn't think that I would need it." said Lyla.

"Oh, never mind. Anthony go out to the car and bring Lyla the guitar." said Eddie. Anthony was Eddie's son. He was very shy and quiet, unlike his father who tended to be loud and bossy. Anthony inherited more of his mother, Rebecca traits. She was quiet and shy too. When Anthony returned back with the guitar, he forgot to grab the guitar pick that was in the gloves department, so he headed back to the car.

"Lord had mercy. How did Anthony forget to get the guitar pick? He should have got that first, than we wouldn't be having this problem," said Eddie muttering to himself. Lyla over heard what Eddie had said about Anthony and was very upset with him. Lyla said a silent prayer before approaching Eddie.

"Help me Jesus," Lyla silently prayed. "Eddie, you have a wonderful son. He's making good grades in school, attends every church service that is occurring, and stays out of trouble. Maybe you shouldn't be so hard on him. He's trying his best," said Lyla with ease. See that didn't go so bad, but how was Eddie taking this. The words pondered in his mind.

"You know what, Lyla? You are absolutely right. My son is a pretty good kid, huh. I raised him well." said Eddie.

"Yeah, you sure did. That is why I thought it was wrong and unfair how you treated him just a few minutes ago." said Lyla.

"Yeah pray for me sister." asked Eddie.

"I sure will. Don't forget to pray for me too." said Lyla.

"I will," responded Eddie. Anthony returned back with both the guitar and the pick. Now they were ready to praise the Lord. The rehearsal turned out great. The children stayed in harmony and Eddie kept his temper. They rehearsed three songs, but decided to sing two on Sunday morning. The parents came on time to pick up their babies, and Eddie, Anthony, and Lyla stayed behind to pick up candy wrappers and other pieces of paper in the church. After cleaning up, Lyla went home to go to bed.

Chapter Twenty-Nine

The sun peeked through the blinds and touched Lyla with her warm embrace. The sun gently woke her up with a soft kiss. Today was so beautiful.

"Good morning sweetie," said Benjamin.

"Good morning," responded Lyla with no babe or sweetie ending. Benjamin didn't pay attention, so he missed her response. He leaned over to give Lyla a kiss, but she jerked away. Lyla was still upset about what happened last night she really wanted things to be done the right way. She wondered when was Benjamin going to purpose to her, so that they could stop this sinning. She knew that her father didn't approve and it was only a matter of time until Rev. Johnson showed it. The telephone rang. "Hello, Benjamin speaking." said Benjamin.

"Hello? Is Lyla there?" asked Rev. Johnson. Lyla didn't know what to do anymore.

"No, she's downstairs cooking big daddy something to eat," said Benjamin. Lyla snatched the phone from Benjamin.

"Hello?" said Lyla.

"Hi sweetie, how are you feeling today?" asked Rev. Johnson.

"Oh, I'm fine daddy. Sorry for what Benjamin said earlier. He's a big jokester," said Lyla.

"Yeah I see. Ha ha ha," said Rev. Johnson sarcastically.

"You called pretty early is everything all right?" asked Lyla.

"Everything is fine. I just wanted to hear my baby's voice that's all." said Rev. Johnson.

"Oh how sweet." said Lyla. "I'm happy you called to check on me, daddy. I love you very much."

"I love you too, sweetie. Are we still having breakfast?" asked Rev. Johnson.

"Of course. Where would you like to go for breakfast?" asked Lyla.

"How about Denny's? We could go there." said Rev. Johnson.

"Denny's sounds great. Should I meet you there?" asked Lyla.

"No. I'll pick you up." said Rev. Johnson. "I want to see that man of yours again and take a real good look at him. When are you two going to get married?"

"Soon father, we're just waiting for the right time that's all no rush." said Lyla. She knew that the topic would be mentioned again.

"Does that man even love you?" asked Rev. Johnson.

"Father, I need to get dressed. We can talk about this later." said Lyla.

"All right, I'll leave it alone for now, but I will bring it up again. Sweetie, you need to know these things." said Rev. Johnson.

"I know father, I know." said Lyla. She took a long shower. Lyla knew that her father was right. He just wanted the best for his baby. Lyla did too, but what did Benjamin want? That question haunted Lyla, because she wasn't sure if Benjamin really loved her or not. Of course, he bought her gifts and took her out to dinner from time to time, but what about the small things like holding hands while walking in the park or reading short passages in a book preferably the Bible, and then talking about them.

The way her father use to do when she was young. He taught her how to enjoy and appreciate the small things in life like flowers and chirping birds. Oh, how Lyla prayed for a man that way, but she had Benjamin: a strong and sexy man with cute dimples. Could she ever see pass the cute smile and hugs without becoming attached? Only the Lord knew. Breakfast with Rev. Johnson was wonderful. He showed Lyla her baby pictures and told her how bad she used to be when she was young.

When Lyla was nine, she broke her father's blue vest on accident and hid in the closet until he came home. He knew she broke it, but he didn't scream at all. Instead they went to the store and bought super glue to glue the pieces together. Those were the good ole' days, when Lyla didn't have any bills or crazy man trouble because she had her father, who was and is her hero and her best friend. Yeah, her father was awesome. They ordered the same food: a cheese steak omelet with a side of rice for Lyla and a side of grits for Al Johnson. Also, some hash browns with two slices of wheat toast, two turkey sausage links and two plates of waffles.

They both could talk a mile a minute. The conversations would make them both laugh and cry. Lyla was enjoying her time with her father and her father was enjoying her company as well. Overall, the breakfast went great and smooth. Rev. Johnson didn't bring up the conversation about marriage and Lyla made sure she didn't lead him on.

Later on that night, Lyla noticed a strange silence in the house. Benjamin had gone out with his boys Benny and Skip to a barbeque party, so she had the whole place to herself.

Weird, why was it so quiet in here? Lately the condo's been quiet. The carpet had not been rolled on and the color had not faded. The pillows on the couch had not been torn or shard and the smell of poop had left. For two days, Lyla has noticed this. Something was wrong with this picture. Someone was missing but whom? Lyla went to the patio and saw nothing. She searched the whole condo. Lyla began to panic. Her dogs were missing, Charlie and Miley were gone! "My babies! Where are my Havanese dogs?" exclaimed Lyla.

She checked the patio again, she couldn't believe this. She sat on the couch to calm down. As she sat down, she noticed a flashing red light on the message machine. "Hello Benjamin. We had picked up the dogs like you requested and brought them to Jojo's Dog Shelter." *Beep.* What? Jojo's Dog Shelter. "I know that boy didn't call the dog shelter." said Lyla. "If he did, only God knew what she would do. Lyla calm yourself, maybe the message was played by mistake, thought Lyla. *Lord please let it be so.*

Benjamin came home around a quarter to seven. Lyla's face was boiling hot she counted to ten to cool down her temper. Benjamin knew that Lyla had found out. He tried to rush toward the bedroom, when Lyla stopped him. Lyla paced herself. She knew that at any moment she would had exploded in fury, but kept her composure. Benjamin was speechless. Where should he began, "I guess you've heard about the Jojo's Dog shelter and is very upset with me. I am sorry Lyla, but the dogs had to go," said Benjamin.

Take deep breaths Lyla. She took deep breaths. "Who gave you the right to send my dogs away? You must have been out of your mind. You need to go down to the Dog's shelter and bring them back," said Lyla.

"No, you need to stop tripping. This is my house and those dogs had to go," said Benjamin. "Think of it as a favor from me to you. Why are you so hostile?"

"Because you didn't ask me to see how I would feel about the situation, you just got up and did what you wanted to do," said Lyla. "We are in a relationship, Benjamin. You just don't make your own decisions and forget about me. You are a very selfish man."

"Well I didn't think it mattered. You weren't here at the time and the dogs were getting on my nerves," said Benjamin. *Like you are getting on my mine* thought Lyla.

"You know what Benjamin. I am not going to get all worked up for you. I was having a good day and will continue to have a good day." said Lyla as she walked away, but in the back of her mind she was thinking of ways to get her dogs back and kicking Benjamin out, exchanging a dog for a dog. Lyla prayed: *Oh Lord, please forgive me for what I just said about Benjamin,* she was only speaking out of pain. Angry, Lyla went in Benjamin and her bedroom, she was too upset to call the room "theirs" to find something that Benjamin deeply cared about to get rid of, but she was out of luck.

Benjamin didn't have anything in the room that she could throw away. There were a few items that she found, but they both liked them so she searched for other things. Giving up now, Lyla stormed out the room and went to the kitchen. She decided not to talk to Benjamin at all. She silently made a salad with smoked ham, shredded mozzarella cheese, and ranch croutons. She used some buttermilk Ranch as the topping. Lyla knew that she should be asking him to leave now, but what was the point of having a relationship if that person couldn't work it out. The *Lord would help her.*

Looking past his shoulders, Benjamin saw Lyla in the kitchen with her back turned to him. "Hey sweetie, would you make me a salad? A brotha is starving," said Benjamin. But Lyla didn't say anything instead she got herself something to drink and went back inside the bedroom. Lyla sense no remorse in Benjamin's voice. He hopped up from the couch and followed Lyla in the bedroom. "You didn't hear what I said when you were in the kitchen?" said Benjamin. "I asked if you could make me a salad. Still Lyla remained silent and ate her salad.

"Fine. I'll make it myself. And you bet not ask for none either," said Benjamin. Lyla was really trying to be humble about this situation, but she wanted to make Benjamin pay. He headed toward the kitchen and took the ingredients that he would need. Mumbling under his breath, Lyla walked in the kitchen behind him. "Oh, now you want to come when you see me in the kitchen," said Benjamin. Lyla placed her salad bowl in the sink and walked away. She wanted to put her bowl in the dishwasher, but Benjamin was in the way so she waited.

Later on that night, Lyla fell asleep while Benjamin spoke to her. She ignored him all the way to this point. In the dark, Benjamin watched Lyla's chest go up and down as she softly breathed. He wanted to hold her, so he leaned closer to her body but she moved. He tried wrapping his legs around her, but she got up from the bed and stretched. "Lyla, I am very sorry. Would you please talk to me?" asked Benjamin. Earlier, he was so caught up in his self that he didn't recognize how hurt Lyla was, but now it was clearly evident. "I don't like it, when you are mad at me. Can we talk about…Lyla raised her hand to silence him and ended the conversation with two words before grabbing a pillow and blanket and sleeping on the couch.

Her eyes appeared as black coals as she the words brought chills down Benjamin's back. The words that Lyla used were: Good night, Benjamin. She slammed the bedroom door behind her. As she lie on the couch, she thought about what had just taken place. Benjamin had wanted to apologize, but she wouldn't let him. She wondered if her heart was that broken or she was so upset that she didn't want to forgive him.

Chapter Thirty

Isn't it funny how God worked everything out? thought Lyla. She arrived at church with a blank mind and still God placed a scripture upon her heart. The scripture was of forgiveness. Lately, Lyla had been holding a grudge against Benjamin. She hadn't talk to him at all. She still couldn't believe what Benjamin did to her, who had asked him to call the dog's shelter in the first place? Lyla took a deep breath and walked inside the church. In the back of her mind, she could hear her father telling her to approach the thrown of grace, the hospital of God that she might be healed.

Before entering the church, she said a silent prayer: "Lord, please give me the strength and courage to teach this class despite of my feelings. Lord you know how hurt I am inside." Forgiveness. What was the key to reconciliation? Lyla baffled with this term of word. "Hello everyone. I am glad that you all are here. Today's lesson would be both enlightened and difficult to speak on, but with God's help I can do it," said Lyla. "Before we begin, let's say a prayer." The scripture was found in Ephesians 4:32, the phrase that Lyla would speak on was "forgiveness," which God had laid on her heart.

What was forgiveness? An act of mercy found between a friend or pretended foe. Many could look at forgiveness as a difficult task because it required a person to lower their standards and become a person of meekness like Jesus Christ, but who could compare themselves to Jesus Christ a sinless man and teacher? Lyla continued on in this matter. She felt that she had preached rather than taught the word, but that was how the words were given to her. What had troubled Lyla so much was Benjamin attitude toward her dogs. It appeared as if the very thing that Lyla cared about and was so happy to see every day—- not saying that Benjamin wasn't important—-didn't mean anything to Benjamin that's why he was so eager to get rid of the dogs.

He had specifically taken away the dogs that Lyla loved. Despite of how she felt, the words still came out strong. Those were some powerful words that you said back there, Lyla" said Brother Robert.

"I know they were," said Lyla. "I was just saying what I felt in my heart." Lately, God has been teaching me about forgiveness and tonight, the words just flowed." said Lyla.

"Oh, I know. God's been dealing with me as well. I need to learn how to forgive some people too." said Brother Robert as he patted Lyla on the back. Before leaving, they said another prayer before going home. Brother Robert had volunteered to close the church out with an ending prayer. "Amen." The bible study group chanted. Lyla gathered her belongings and went outside. The moon was half-hidden behind some dark clouds and a glimpse of a star sparkled.

Maybe there was hope for her, for them, for Benjamin. She prayed. She hoped. She wished. When Lyla got home, the whole house was silent and dark. Benjamin was sleeping on the couch with a hand resting on his chest holding the remote control. A couple of beer bottles were scattered on the round table. Lyla softly kissed Benjamin's forehead. The fights weren't worth the silence that had fallen on them. As Lyla walked away, Benjamin smiled and opened his eyes.

He followed Lyla in the bedroom. "Oh, you startled me. I thought that you were asleep," grasped Lyla.

"I was sleeping, but your lips woke me up," he smiled again.

"I am sorry for ignoring you. I just needed to clear my mind. Do you forgive me?" asked Lyla.

"No, I should be the one asking for your forgiveness. What I did with the dogs wasn't cool. I'm sorry. Do you forgive me?" asked Benjamin.

"Yes, only if you promise to bring them back to me. I forgive you. I hate it when we don't talk to one another, I feel this distance between us, "said Lyla. Benjamin leaned over and gave Lyla a hug, he was happy to hold her again. Being a sentimental moment, Lyla really wanted to ask Benjamin about proposal, but didn't know how. Should she just say it or hint it? She felt as though time was running out.

"Of course, Lyla. Whatever you say." said Benjamin, but he never kept his word. Lyla dogs were still gone.

The children were very happy to see Lyla and she was happy to see them too. She enjoyed spending time with the youths, especially the youth choir. They were always eager to sing a song for the Lord. Today, the children were going to sing 'This Little Light of Mine' and 'Jesus Loves Me'. Lyla could not wait to lead the choir. The presence of the Lord would surely fall on this place. They sung like angels. The words had touched Lyla's soul. She had been going through a lot that week and needed to hear those words of comfort.

"Oh, my darlings. Everyone sounded so precious," said Lyla with tears in her eyes. A child noticed Lyla's tears and gently consoled her.

"Teacher, why are you crying?" asked the child. "Don't you know that God is a healer and nothing is impossible for him? Let your light shine, for your last name does end with Star," said the child who gave Lyla a sense of relief and comfort. Who would have known that God would use a small child to encourage her? Then again, she needed a loving father.

"Well, that's all for today. Everyone did excellent," said Lyla, as she began to gather her purse and car keys. Outside in the church parking lot, parents and elders wait in their cars for their child or children, but the girl that had spoken to Lyla wasn't in any rush. Before leaving, she turned around and gave Lyla a bear hug. "Bye, Ms. Star. Have a good night and remember that God loves you," said the young child.

"Bye, um...what's your name?" asked Lyla.

"Angel, my name is Angel," the child smiled again and waved good bye.

Chapter Thirty-One

As Lyla drove home, she couldn't help but to think of Angel and how precious she was. Lyla was grateful to have met her. She wondered how Angel knew that she was struggling. Her name definitely fitted her description. She was an angel that was sent for Lyla. Once she approached the driveway, she said another silent prayer before going inside, how she wished that everything between Benjamin and herself could be the same but God was always two steps ahead of her and worked everything out.

Lyla was in such a haze that she didn't recognized how quickly she arrived at home. It was only eight forty-five p.m., still she was happy to be home early to spend more time with Benjamin. As she took the key out of the ignition, she opened the car door and walked toward the front door. The condo was silenced. "Benjamin...are you here?" asked Lyla as she walked inside the living room to turn on the light, she stopped when she saw some white powder lined horizontal on a piece of brown cardboard.

Her mouth had dropped. She didn't know that Benjamin was into that kind of stuff. Her father had warned her about guys like him, she could hear one of her father's lectured stanzas: *Be careful who you let in your home. There are good people and bad people in life and you don't ever want* to associate yourself with a bad person. Especially one that does cocaine, a person like this is possessed and does things that are very harmful to others.

Lyla felt stuck and afraid. She heard Benjamin sneezed and jumped a little, she stood in the middle of the room. What should she do now? Her heart was beating fast *boom-boom, boom-boom* as she stood there frozen. She had to act fast, before Benjamin saw her. Slowly taking her car keys out of her pocket, she tip-toed to the door and reached for the door knob. Too late! Lyla turned around when Benjamin called her name. He snorted one line on the cardboard, before saying anything else.

"And where do you think you're going?" asked Benjamin wiping his nose with the back of his hand.

"Nowhere, sweetie. I was just going outside for some fresh air," said Lyla placing the key back into her pocket.

"Do you think I am dumb? I saw your keys in your hand. You were trying to leave me, "said Benjamin standing up now.

"No I wasn't. I just got home from church and had the keys in my hand when I unlocked the door to come in," said Lyla shaking a little.

"Liar!" he said approaching her. "I know you were trying to leave me," they stood face to face of each other, when she noticed a risen left hand smacking her. She fell face down to the floor. He raised his foot to kick her from underneath; he slapped her again and unbuckled his leather black belt.

"Stop Benjamin! You're hurting me!" she begged and pleaded, but he showed no mercy. As Benjamin snatched his belt from the last belt loop, he wrapped the belt buckle around his fist and beat Lyla. She squirmed and wiggled to keep from feeling the lashes and kicked him in the chest. That angered Benjamin. He picked her up from the floor and carried her from the waist on his shoulders. Lyla pouched his back with her petite fists and screamed out the words: HELP ME! As they walked into the dark bedroom, he threw her on the bed, ripped off her clothes and unfastened his zipper.

He wore nothing underneath and stroked the excitement that he had hidden away in his pants. As the night fell, tears rolled down Lyla's face and her throat became hoarse from screaming. Benjamin sat up in bed with a cigarette in his mouth. He mumbled some words as he searched the room for his pants. "Listen," he said inhaling the smoke. "I'm leaving to clear my mind," his voice sounded muffled with the cigarette hanging from his lips. "Don't worry about me, I would be in good hands, good satin sheets...hell even some good panties." He found a white T-shirt on the dresser and opened the drawer for white socks.

His brown leather shoes were placed by the door, making his departure simple and easy. "So don't wait up." Lyla was silent. She couldn't wait for him to leave the house. Once outside, he called Nina up and told her that he was ready to go.

"Ok, I would be there soon!" said Nina shouting a little.

"Lyla was asleep when I came out here, don't wake her up with your loud mouth," said Benjamin putting another cigarette in his mouth. Nina pulled up in her blue Supreme Cutlass.

"I am here. You don't need that, honey. I would keep you warmer than that filtered Newport, said Nina as he stepped inside the car.

"We will see. Let's get out of here," said Benjamin placing the un-lighted cigarette in his front right jean pocket.

Chapter Thirty-Two

Lyla was awakening by a huge thunder. Boom! Her face was still in pain from last night blows of Benjamin's fists. He had damaged her face completely and her body ached form his forced staff within her temple; the very body that she was given to honor and worship God. She felt robbed both internally and externally and didn't want to wake up to face the world. The thought of even seeing herself in the mirror made her felt ashamed and disgraced.

Lyla didn't move. She laid in the bed perfectly still, with her ached body and her broken heart. How could the man she loved hurt, beat and rob her all the same time? The tears began to form out of her sad brown eyes. As she laid there to think about her life, she was startled when she heard the black portable phone ring by the bed. The phone rang again. She was hesitating to pick up the phone, she feared the caller might be Benjamin to remind Lyla of the power that he had over her.

The phone rang a third time. Lyla watched the phone as it rang and rang. Who could be calling her? She took a deep breath and picked up the phone. "Hello?" she whispered.

"Hello, Lyla? This is your father. Are you all right?" asked Rev. Johnson on the other line. "Hello? Lyla?"

She knew that her swollen jaw would have made it impossible for her to speak clearly, so she pronounced every syllable in every word she spoke. "Lyla answer me. Are you all right?"

"Hel-lo dad. I-am-fine," she said in a soft whisper.

"Lyla, I can barely hear you. Hold on for a minute...he turned up the volume. "There." The volume was turned to the maximum. "Lyla, what did you say? Could you repeat that? Lyla took another deep breath and repeated the words that she said before.

"Hel-lo dad. I-am-fine," said Lyla again in a soft whisper. When she didn't hear a respond from him, she used all her strength to speak much louder, but again only a whisper came out.

"Lyla, I still can't hear you. I would be there soon." This wasn't like her at all. Normally, she was perked and happy to hear her father's voice, when she was in high spirit. Now she was beaten pretty badly and her right cheek hurt with every word she spoke. Despite her pain, she had another issue that she had to worry about: hiding the bruises from her father. She had bruises and black marks on a few places on her body, not including her face. Benjamin had kicked her in the stomach, leaving an imprint of a tennis size black mark above the navel.

Her arms and legs revealed red welts from the lash of Benjamin's belt and her behind felted numb in the center. She looked at the time on the portable phone. It was a quarter 'til twelve. She finished the conversation with her father twenty minutes ago. He should be here soon. Lyla slowly raised herself up from the bed. She had been holding her urine in for a while and felt her kidney began to burst. "Oh, I-am-in-so-much-pain," her voice barely loud. As she arose from the cotton sheets, her foot hit the floor finding their way in the fluffy black slippers.

She stood up and cried as she walked toward the bathroom, she mumbled the word *ouch* as she placed one foot after another. When she walked inside the bathroom, she almost fainted when she saw her reflection in the mirror, but held on to the sink. She found the toilet. She couldn't recognize her own face. Her hair was dismantled and her skin looked pale, how much longer did she have before she heard the door bell rung or an anxious knock on the red wooden door?

Lyla didn't know. How could see comb her hair, wash her face, brush her teeth, bath herself and hide the bruises all at the same time? Lyla didn't know. She washed her hands, still thinking to herself, when she heard the doorbell rung following three aggressive knocks on the door. If that didn't grab her attention, the next alternative would have as her father called out her name.

"Lyla! Lyla open up the door now!" She heard her father's voice. She knew there was no running from the truth this time, taking her third breath she tip-toed toward the front door with her messy hair and busted face and reached the doorknob and saw her father down on his knees as he beheld the image of his broken daughter, while rain poured down off his hurt face.

Meanwhile, Benjamin and Nina were getting ready to blow each other mind with a *Ka-Pow* here and an *Ah* there. The setting was perfect as he came closer to her. The lights had been turned low in Nina's apartment as she played a melody from Kenny G in the background. They have been dating for about four months now. The relationship was unexpected, it just happened. One day they were talking and drinking tequilas when *wham!* They hooked up. Benjamin brought excitement in Nina's life that she had never felt before...she was so alive!

There was no way she would allow Lyla to mess this up for her. Benjamin had been so good to her and her body, plus it was time for him to get a real woman anyway. "I have been anticipated all night and now we are together again for a second round, "said Nina rubbing his leg.

"You know you could go farther than that if you like? I am all yours," said Benjamin taking off his shirt.

"Do you remember what happened last time?" asked Nina. "We were so into it that you almost exploded in the condom while being inside. Babe, all I am saying is that we need to slow down."

"I know, but with Lyla trippin' every day. I can't control this urgency and stress inside. I need you babe and I mean for real this time," said Benjamin smiling.

"Don't tell me, Benjamin. Are you referring to...?"

"Yes," he answered. "Tonight there will be no protection; just raw skin."

Chapter Thirty-Three

"Lyla, what happened to your face?" asked Rev. Johnson as rain continued to moisture the grass and her father's dark corduroys. He nodded his head in sadness. "Did that wanna-be hood boyfriend of yours do this to you?'

"Dad! It-wasn't-his-fault, we-got-into-an-argument," said Lyla as she kept her eyes to the floor.

"Lord, have mercy. Let me come in to see what kind of argument this was." He grabbed onto the slippery cold door knob to lift himself up and waddled into the house. He reached for Lyla's hand, but she quickly grasped when she felt his cold touch. The rain had wrinkled and frozen his fingers she pointed toward the hall closet. He found some dry towels. As he walked to the closet, he grabbed two face towels: one for his hands and the other for his daughter's face. He wet the towel with warm water before giving in to Lyla.

"You should put the towel on your cheek, honey." The swelling may go down some," said Rev. Johnson while reaching for her hand a second time to sit on the navy colored love sit sofa. "When did this happen?"

"Last-night-after-church, I-came-home-and-he...," he raised his hand to silence her.

"Sweetie, I can tell you are swore and tired. Why don't we talk about this some other time," said Rev. Johnson.

"I-am-fine-father. Let-me-finish-the-story-so-here-I-was-coming-home-and-he," again he raised his hand.

"Honey, don't stress yourself. By bringing up the story, you would become upset and God knows how I would react," Rev. Johnson said. "How about this. We walk back to your bedroom. I fluff you up with several soft pillows and make you a bowl of hot chicken noodle soup. How does that sound?"

"Good, but-dad-what-about-my-teens-session-tonight?" asked Lyla.

"I would handle that sweetie. Why don't you get some rest," he said.

"But, but-dad-I-told-the-teens-that-I-would-oh-never mind. You-are-right, I-need-to-rest," she said giving into his orders. How could she argue with him? He was right and Lyla knew it. Her father's hand was warm again. He led her into the bedroom and onto the queen size bed. Several pillows were positioned behind her as she laid down while stretching her legs. She wondered what was wrong with her father. He didn't raise his voice at all and yet she was frightened to know what was to come of this situation.

Her father has assured her that everything would be all right, but she had the hardest time believing it. Her mind would go back on thoughts of Benjamin's wrath. "Are you comfortable? Do you need any more pillows?" her father remained at ease. He wasn't happy seeing his daughter this way, but he knew that vengeance was the Lord's and it wasn't up to him to fight back with weapons, but with prayer. And that was all he could do at that moment, make the chicken noodle soup and pray all day long.

When the soup was ready, he gently woke Lyla up with a soft tap on the shoulders. "Honey, your soup is ready," Rev. Johnson said. He placed all items on a platter: a bowl of chicken noodle soup with saltine crackers with a nice cold lemon tea. On her right side, he placed a small silver spoon and on her left side, a folded clean napkin. Lyla had fallen asleep after he fluffed the last pillow. The soup was the only meal she had all day. Her father had a feeling she would only eat soup, so he made two cans worth.

After eating the first bowl of soup, she gave her father the number for her teens' sessions to cancel the meeting. Her heart was unhappy because she was looking so forward with teaching tonight. Her father understood her pain, but she needed to rest. He took the number from her. He would dial once she was asleep, which didn't take long. Her eye lids had closed after a few bits of her second bowl. She still looked beautiful, as she breathed slowly in and out. Her father used her phone and dialed the number.

"Hello, is this the teen session facility that was scheduled for Lyla Johnson?" Someone answered on the other end.

"Yes. Hello. My name is Marge. Sorry, could you repeat that Sir?" She sounded about eighteen years old.

"I am calling in regards to my daughter's teens' session meeting," said Rev. Johnson.

"What is your daughter's name?" she asked.

"Lyla Johnson," he replied.

"Oh, that's a pretty name, Sir. Could you wait, while I check the teens' schedule?" she asked.

"Yes," he said.

"Sir? I do have a teens' session for Lyla Johnson tonight. Did she want to reschedule her meeting?" she asked.

"Yes, that would be nice. She's a little ill and need to stay home to rest." said Rev. Johnson.

"I understand. No worries. What date would she like to schedule it, Sir?" asked the girl.

"I don't know. When she is well, I would have her call you back." said Rev. Johnson.

"All right. I hope she gets better soon. Have a blessed day." she said.

"Thank you and you have a blessed day as well," he hanged up the black portable phone and smiled. He figured everyone wasn't crazy; there were still some good people in the world.

Chapter Thirty-Four

As weeks went by, Lyla had slowly recovered from her pain. Her father would help her bathed and get dressed every day, in which she appreciated. But wasn't ready to become completely redeemed of her short comings. She had already made it up in her mind. The first chance she got at her father's place, she would celebrate. He figured being in a new environment would protect her. She gathered some clothes mostly miniskirts, some under garments and a few clean tops.

She also packed a pair of sweat pants just in case. While packing, she looked under the bathroom sink for Benjamin's liquor stash: a half of patron, a full bottle of Vodka and white wine. Lyla couldn't believe how the party happened so quickly. First she called Nina to come over her father's house for some girls' fun, when Nina invited Benjamin to come along. They were discussing their exciting intermingling that had taken place while back. Next, Benny and Skip came crashing through when they saw cars parked all in the driveway.

Lyla was looking good in her leopard mini-skirt and strapless top. She was surprised to see Benjamin coming in with Nina. She wasn't in the mood in seeing his face after what he did to her. It took a miracle and she recovered from her injuries by her father's supplication and his prayers.

"Hey girl! Oh I love that skirt," said Nina eyeing Lyla's skirt up and down. Nina wore a hot pink mini-skirt a buttoned down jacket that matched. Lyla didn't respond. She stared at Benjamin as he walked over to where Benny and Skip had sat. He wore some black jeans and a white T-shirt.

"Why did you bring him here, Nina? This is supposed to be a girls' party," said Lyla with swollen eyes. Apparently the scars had not left yet. Nina looked around the room, she noticed all girls at the party.

"Oh, I didn't know. I am sorry. If you want us to leave I understand," she said as she slowly walked toward Benjamin.

"Us? Nina what are you talking about?" Lyla began to follow Nina when her father came home.

"Lyla!" she could hear the fury in his voice.

"Yes, father."

"Who are all these girls in my house with liquor on their breath? Lyla took a deep breath.

"Just some friends from my neighborhood..."

"And who is sitting on my couch?" Again, Lyla tried to speak.

"Some of Nina's friends, dad. Please don't go...in there, she finished too late.

"That wanna-be gangster! Everybody get out of my house now!" The crowd of girls didn't hear him, so he screamed louder. "Get out now, before I call the police." The girls didn't hesitate this time, they ran out. Benjamin was on the couch whispering something in Nina's ear that made her giggled, maybe something negative about Lyla, while Benny and Skip was trying to get one of the girls' numbers.

"Say Ma, you look good in those jeans. How about some company tonight? I won't bite," said Benny.

"Yeah, he won't...won't bite," shuttered Skip right behind him as they followed the two tall brunettes out the door.

"I am going to count to three. If I get to three and you are still here," her father pointed to Benjamin. "I would call the police on you."

"Benjamin lets go," said Nina holding his hand and pulling him up to his feet. Benjamin stood up. Lyla watched as Nina held on to his hand, that theft. But she could have him. He knew what he would be missing if Lyla never came home, some good loving. He would be back. Once everyone left, Lyla and her father got into an argument. "You have some nerve throwing a party in my house, while I was away," he said. "What was you thinking, Lyla?"

"Freedom, I guess. Dad, I appreciate your help when I needed you, but now I am well and just wanted to have some fun," she said picking up the red plastic cups off the table and floor to throw into the trash. A few Chex Mix was scattered on the carpet and someone spelled a small drop of Vodka on the kitchen counter. Lyla made sure to clean that up. Other than that, the house wasn't completely destroyed or out of order.

"As long as you are under my roof, you would abide by my rules," Rev. Johnson said.

"Then maybe I should leave," she said. "I wasn't giving you anything, but a headache anyway."

"That is completely up to you, but if you leave now, you cannot come back. I would not allow such sinful living in my house. And you could forget about coming back to the firm, young lady. Your attitude is unacceptable," Rev. Johnson said.

"Well I guess I'll go, then," she said as she gathered her belongings. Her father watched her as she slide on a pair of sweat pants and wore a thin black jacket that someone had left to cover up her top. Before stepping out the door, her father gave her a business card that read: **Taxi Services** and told her to ask for Joseph.

The white Porsche that she had before was gone because that wannabe gangster forgot to pay the monthly car note, which they were five months behind. With the card in her hand, she searched for her cellular to dial the number. Her father gave her his portable and said "It's a lot cheaper." Lyla looked at the time on the phone. It was six fifteen p.m. and her minutes wouldn't be free for another forty-five minutes: seven o'clock. She dialed the number and asked for Joseph like her father ordered.

Chapter Thirty-Five

"Hello, can I speak to Joseph?" asked Lyla.
"Hello, this is Joseph speaking," he said. In a number of minutes he came by, slowly driving up to the curb. She walked outside to a boisterous wind and a heavy clouds. The sky looked threatening and dark. She placed her duffle bag in the trunk and asked Joseph if he could go by 42nd Street to her condo to grab some extra things.

"No problem," he said as he drove away. Her eyes looked sad as she departed from her father. She knew that leaving would be best for the both of them. They arrived at the condo. Again, she asked if he could stay while she gathered some things.

"No problem," he said as before. She found her keys and unlocked the door. She didn't plan to stay long. She walked straight to her bedroom. She opened the door. She was startled. Before her, was a motion of sudden movements going on in her bed. The blankets had hidden the intruder's face, so she didn't know who it could be, but when she saw the hot pink mini-skirt on the floor and a pair of black jeans on top of the brown wooden dresser. She knew the rest and snatched the covers off them.

While Nina rode, Benjamin laid on his back. They both stood speechless in the act," busted was the only word that

Lyla could think of. She was done with both Benjamin and Nina, if they wanted to sneak around to be together then let it be. Lyla didn't need the headache.

In silence, she walked to the closet and grabbed some more clothes and shoes. She went to the bathroom to change into a white creamy blouse and black slacks. The rain outside convinced her to change from her mini-skirt into something much warmer perhaps some jeans would had work, but she didn't want to wear anything that reminded her of Benjamin.

Since that was the last thing he wore before getting it on. Therefore, the slacks would work perfectly. The other day, she took out the rest of the money she had in her saving account: two-hundred dollars. She hidden the money in a small jewelry box with a silver lock. She took the box and rushed outside. Joseph waited patiently outside. He wasn't in any rush at all. She ran outside, holding an umbrella she found around the house as she exited the condo.

"Find everything you need?" he asked as Lyla closed the door.

"Yes and some other things that I wasn't ready for," said Lyla shivering a little. He turned on the heat.

"Good. So where are you heading to now?" he asked.

"Anywhere," she just wanted to leave town and escape this madness. "A hotel would work."

"A hotel it is," he said and drove far out into a neighborhood that appeared strange to Lyla. She had never driven in this part of town. "Welcome to the Golden Capri Hotel."

Chapter Thirty-Six

At times, Lyla would found herself reminiscing about what happened prior to her stay at the hotel. Lyla couldn't believe that all that had happened to her with her father, boyfriend and Ex best friend. She was glad that she left, but wished that things could have turned out better for everyone.

It had been two weeks and Lyla still hadn't met all the guests that lived in the hotel. She wasn't obligated to meet anyone. She just wanted to be familiar with faces that would be coming and going out of this place, since this would be her new home. Today, she met Mrs. Golden, an elderly woman that was slightly up there. She told Lyla the truth, Lyla had become such a coward to ever witness again, which Lyla didn't respond at all. She needed that healing again, called faith to help her.

If given the opportunity to preach again, would she? Lyla didn't know. She saw herself as an unfinished map, clueless and lost as she wanted to be. Beside Mrs. Golden was her grandson, Thomas what a cutie pie. He had the cutest face like that of a cabbage doll, curly thread black hair and dimples. To be eight years old, Thomas was very strong. He flexed to show off his muscles; wasn't Lyla impressed.

She had to focus on repaying Valerie back. Lyla still didn't have a job and was trying to get re-hired at her dad's firm, but he hasn't called her. As Lyla walked around in her room waiting for her dad to call, she became impatient and headed to the lobby downstairs. At the lobby, Valerie was behind the desk smiling about something that had just happened.

"Hey Valerie. What are you smiling about? asked Lyla as she walked closer to her.

"Oh, two newlyweds just came in with their "Just Married" matching shirts and their smiling faces. They are truly in love," said Valerie gleefully.

Rev. Johnson

While preaching another great sermon, Reverend Johnson couldn't help but to think about his daughter, Lyla. It had been awhile since they last spoke to each other. He didn't remember exactly how long it had been. As he took his seat, he heard the congregation clapping their hands and chanting "Amen!" His spirit was moved by the applauses, but his mind would drift off on his baby again. Where could she be now?

After the applauses, Rev. Johnson stepped to the podium to close out with the benediction and remarks. His mind was still troubled with the absence of his daughter that he had forgotten to call for discipleship and alter prayer. He was reminded afterwards by brother and deacon, Stokes. "Hey Pastor Johnson, are you all right?" asked David.

"Hello Deacon Stokes. Not completely. But I know that God is going to work it out." said Rev. Johnson.

"That's right. He can handle anything. Just continue to trust Him, pastor. He knows and understands. Is there anything that I could pray for or someone?" asked David.

"Yes. Pray for my daughter that she will find her way back home and my strength in the Lord." said Rev. Johnson.

"I will, pastor. Be blessed." Reverend Johnson smiled at Brother Stokes. He sure would make a fine son-in-law one day.

Nina

As she rubbed her stomach, Nina was reminded of her actions that she done with Benjamin that resulted in such loneliness. Benjamin didn't even know that Nina was pregnant. Before she could even tell him, they get into an argument and she left. She couldn't continue to hurt Lyla the way she did in the past. That was why the two broke up. Again, she rubbed her belly. Nina was about seven months now. She still couldn't believe that she was pregnant.

She should have known that eventually she would have become pregnant with her free practices with Benjamin. And yet, she still couldn't believe it. Then again, one did reap what they sown for Nina it was Benjamin's child. She began to think of names. If Nina had a boy, she might name him Benji and for a girl Benja, both are very pretty. Times like these, Nina wished that she and Lyla were talking to one another. She would rather asked Lyla about the names, than Benjamin anyway.

David

Still astonished, David couldn't believe that this day had come to pass. He had always loved Lyla. Her confidence and knowledge of the Lord, the way she helped so many people who were discouraged and alone and the compassion that many had saw in her big brown eyes and that curly hair of hers. David had fallen in love with her anointing, the Holy Ghost power that abided.

If only she knew the power that was in her. He still couldn't believe that she wouldn't go to church with him, when he asked her. The response she gave him came as strange. If he remembered correctly, she was the one that use to both invite and encourage people to come out, even persuaded David to come out and fellowship. Now she looked lost and alone, he noticed this while looking into her eyes. David cared about his lost darling. He would pray for her. He would stand by her. He loved her and never stopped.

Chapter Thirty-Seven

Meanwhile, Lyla found herself thinking about Benjamin. She missed his voice, his smile, even some of the fights they use to have with one another. Oh how she missed him, but she couldn't go back. She couldn't continue to play the fool, while he lied and cheated on her. She was better off staying at this hotel alone, than with a sinner. But can she judge Benjamin? Wasn't she a sinner for being and sleeping with a man that wasn't her husband, yes?

Lyla has sinned against God, defiled her body, fought with her father, and ran away from the church. She could feel some tears began to fall down her face. In her inner soul, Lyla wanted things to change in her life. She wanted to fall back in love with the Lord and live only for Him. She wanted to respect her body and get back into relations with her father. She wanted to attend church again without feeling so broken inside. She wanted a renewed spirit and a second chance.

David

As he reviewed several documents of staying and leaving tenants, David began to think about Lyla. Lately, he had been praying for her. David prayed that she would find peace and rest in her life. He prayed that she would smile again and be filled with happiness like before. David paused. Before he began to do anything else, he searched left and right to see if anyone was present in the lobby with him. Either way, David would have still prayed because prayer worked.

He said a quiet prayer. *Lord, what should I do to encourage Lyla more and help her?* He asked in Jesus name. The Lord heard him and directed his attention to today's calendar. David was confused. Today was Wednesday...*And?* David gave up. Again, David prayed. *Holy Spirit, can you just tell me please?* The room was silent. Again, David stared at the calendar that had today's date.

Staring hard now, the date became a mere image, when out of nowhere the word: *Wednesday* stood out to him. The word stood out like the word had been high-lighted, *Wednesday*. David glanced at his watch. The time was fifteen minutes 'til six. He had been in the Golden Capri lobby since this morning. He looked outside, the parking lot was dark. Oh, David had to leave to make it to Bible Study tonight. Wait. That was it!

David could invite Lyla to Bible Study. Thank you, Lord. He took the stairs to the second floor and headed to Lyla's room. Lyla didn't know where to start? Lyla had been out of fellowship with God, her father and the church for so long that she really didn't know where to begin. Again, she found herself lost and confused. She didn't know what to do. Lyla put her head in her hands and looked down.

Out of nowhere, she heard a knock at the door. She wondered who this could be. "Hello?" asked Lyla. Outside the door, David hummed a song *Thank you Lord for all you done for me* that he didn't hear her. He knocked again. "Hello? Is anyone out there?" asked Lyla again, but this time a little louder. "Hello, Lyla? Are you in there?" asked David. Lyla jumped up, when she heard his voice.

She didn't want David to see her so down, she rushed to the bathroom and wipe the tears away from her eyes. She opened the door, before David could knock again. "Hello David. How are you?" asked Lyla.

"Oh, I'm doing well. Is this a good or bad time for you?" asked David.

"To be honest with you, David. I was having a bad day before you came. Now I am feeling a little better." said Lyla.

"Good. I am glad to hear that. Hey, I was wondering if you would like to come to Bible Study with me tonight?" asked David.

"Oh, I don't know David. It has been such a long time for me since I have been. I'm sorry, David." said Lyla.

"No problem. I know that on some days we have to rest our mind and body. Maybe some other time. Have a good night." said David.

"You do the same." said Lyla. Again, she missed the opportunity to go to church. Why was it so hard to submit? Lyla headed back to her room. She wondered what it would take for her to walk into the sanctuary. As she entered the room, she silently closed the door behind her but didn't lock it. She walked to her bed to pick up the phone. She was hungry and didn't know what to get.

Chapter Thirty-Eight

Leaving the Pure of Heart church, David headed back to the hotel to make sure that he put away all the documents that he had earlier. When he got there, the front desk was clean and all the documents that he had were gone. Good. He was a little bit worried. Now that he was there at the hotel, he wondered what Lyla was doing. Maybe she was in her room or out and about. He didn't know, but he would like to find out.

About to pick up the desk phone to call her, he heard a voice in his spirit that said *walk to her room*. David obeyed and put the phone back on the receiver. He headed to her room and knocked on the door. Around the third knock, the door slowly opened. David was welcome to Lyla sitting on her bed, thinking to herself. The expression on her face gave David this idea. He stood by the door before walking in.

Lyla saw him and invited him in to her room. "So how was Bible Study?" asked Lyla, still trying to figure out what to eat.

"Oh, Bible Study was good. I wished you would have come, though. You would have really been blessed." said David as he sat on the bed and saw the pictures of her puppies.

"I bet. Now I wished that I would have come. I was only acting out of stubbornness. I should have gone when you had invited me," said Lyla.

"Don't beat yourself up. There is always Sunday mornings," said David with a slight smirk on his face. "You are coming to the Sunday service, right?" Lyla's face felt hot; she quickly turned her head away. "Lyla, what's wrong?" She ignored the question and responded with another question changing the topic.

"Have you eaten yet, David? I was thinking about ordering some Chinese or something." said Lyla. Again, she hid herself from David. He was hurt by this. Didn't she know that David wanted to be there for her; that he loved her?

"You can order whatever you like. I am about to go home and make a nice hot cup of vanilla cappuccino." said David as he left Lyla's room.

"Oh, that sounds nice. Can I come along with you?" asked Lyla. Now David quickly turned his head away. He couldn't leave without telling her something.

"Not tonight. Maybe some other time," said David as he closed the door behind him. Lyla was quiet, things didn't go the way she hoped. She really wanted to spend some time with him. As David exited Lyla's room, he headed toward the stairs to enter the hotel lobby.

Upstairs in her room, Lyla was still upset with what just happened. David only wanted to help her, but she kept pushing him away. Why did she do that? She couldn't bare having David mad at her. She wanted to make things right. Lyla decided to apologize to him for being so rude. She got her room key and pocket book before leaving the room. She figured after apologizing to David, she could stop by the dining area to see what they had to eat.

He saw a girl rubbing her belly standing by the front desk. He spoke out loud so he wouldn't startle the unknown woman. "Hello, may I help you?" asked David walking behind the counter.

"Oh, Hi. My name is Nina. Do you know if Lyla is here?" asked Nina.

"Yes, she is here. Are you a friend or relative? I don't think she would be pleased if a random stranger just appeared at her door." said David.

"Well...we use to be best friends in the past. Now she will not speak to me, so to answer your question, ex-friend." said Nina.

"I can see that you are expecting soon. I bet your husband is very proud?" asked David. "Would you like for me to call Lyla for you?"

"No. I have been trying to get the nerve to call her myself, but I don't think she would answer," said Nina. On that note, she reached in her purse to pull out a pen and a piece of paper. She began to scribble down her name and her number. Nina handed David her number and told him to have Lyla call her anytime, when Lyla showed up out of nowhere.

As she exit the elevators, she walked toward the lobby and found an unexpected guest given David a small piece of paper. The girl's last words were: call her any time, I will be waiting to hear from...

"Stop right there, missy!" yelled Lyla. "What do you think you are doing? Again, you try to take something that doesn't belong to you."

"Lyla...Hi. I was just giving my number to this guy so he could give it to you. I figured you wouldn't want to talk to me over the phone." said Nina. Lyla wasn't buying it. She knew what Nina was doing. Lyla didn't say another word. She headed to the dining area. Nina became speechless, as David watched both women depart once more. Now he knew why, Nina said "ex-friends." Whatever happened in the past had angered Lyla that she just left. "I appreciate you trying to help me, but I think it is best that I leave now." said Nina, again rubbing her stomach.

David wanted to say something to her that would lift up her spirit, but he was at loss for words. The only word that seemed to appear in his mind was *prayer*, which was the only thing that he could do at this point. David would pray that Lyla would be kind to Nina and that Nina would stop being so hard on herself. David noticed how quickly she defended herself, when Lyla saw both him and her together. Again, he wondered what was under Lyla's skin.

Lately, she refused to go to church with him or at all and then she got these strange expressions on her face like: why was he inviting me to go to church again? Surely, she has changed and was not the same person that he thought he knew. Times like these, he looked for guidance from his shepherd and pastor, Rev. Johnson.

Chapter Thirty-Nine

Pastor Johnson always said that David could talk to him, if ever he felt confused or uncertain about something or *someone*. David decided to call the Reverend first to see if he was free to talk, before coming unexpectedly at the Lord's house. He figured that the pastor would be busy with other things, like church documents or prayer requests from fellow members. David didn't want to appear so needed, but he didn't know what to do.

He called the church phone first on his cell to see if anyone would answer, but he got the voicemail. Again David called the church phone. During this time, Pastor was reviewing some church documents, mainly the attendance sheet. Pastor Johnson was pleased to see that majority of the church invited at least two people to church service. Praise the Lord! Only focusing on the church log, Pastor Johnson completely missed the loud phone calls. David, on the other hand was persistent that he called one more time.

He was not going to give up quickly. David called one last time. He nearly dropped the phone, when he heard the Pastor's voice on the other line. "Hello, Reverend Johnson speaking?" said Rev. Johnson.

"Pastor Johnson this is Brother David how are you today?" asked David in a quick slur.

"David, are you all right? Why are you talking fast?" asked Rev. Johnson.

"Pastor, I must speak with you. It is very important." said David.

"All right. How fast can you get here? I will be in my office, waiting for you." Finally, David got in contact with Rev. Johnson. After talking to him over the phone, pastor invited David to stopped by the church so that they could chat. Rev. Johnson could sense such urgency in David's voice. David needed some advice from his pastoral father. When David arrived at Pure of Heart, he saw that the pastor's office door was opened.

Rev. Johnson met David by the door and greeted him with a warm hug. "Oh, pastor Johnson. I don't know what to do anymore. I need help!" said David.

"Brother David, calm down. Take a deep breath," said Pastor Johnson. He picked up a pen and pad that he had on his desk. Being a pastor, Reverend Johnson was use to writing things down to remember them later on. But after David got through sharing his story, Rev. Johnson would remember everything. "All right David. Are you ready to tell me what happened?" asked Rev. Johnson as he wrote down today's date and time.

"Yes, pastor Johnson. I am ready." David took another deep breath. "All right. Here it goes." As David began to tell Pastor Johnson what bothered him, the last words that David said were: the girl that I am talking about, is not only beautiful and intelligent, but is a true blessing from God. Her name is Lyla and I love her! Rev. Johnson didn't know how to respond, when David told him that the girl he loved was his daughter, Lyla. He was speechless.

"Pastor Johnson are you all right? You stopped writing when I said: Lyla" asked David.

"Brother David. The girl that you spoke of is my daughter. I have been praying for her. We were in this argument, when she left my house. I haven't heard from her in a while." said Rev. Johnson. After hearing those words, David became speechless. He was both glad and surprised that the Pastor knew the girl, that she was his daughter. But surprised when the two were in some kind of fight, an argument the pastor said.

"Wow! Look how God work this out. Who would have known that I would mention your daughter and that you would be this speechless? Yes, the Lord is good. Pastor Johnson, you know what you have to do? Pray to the Lord for guidance and call your daughter." said David.

'Where is she, exactly?" asked Rev. Johnson.

"She is at the Golden Capri hotel. She has been staying there for a couple of months. Here is the number, call her." said David. Reverend Johnson took the number from David that was written on a small white card.

"Thank you, David. I will call her in the morning" said Rev. Johnson as he leaned over to give David a hug.

As Rev. Johnson twirled the small white card in his hand, his mind fell on his daughter. Still in amazement, he thought of words to say to her. "Hello daughter...he said in a stern voice, or what about "Hi baby, how's my daughter doing?" Rev. Johnson signed. *Lord, what should I say to my child?* He prayed before picking up the phone. After the conversation with David, Rev. Johnson drove home contemplating on what to say. He looked at his wrist watch, a quarter 'til eleven. His eyes were beginning to feel heavy. He decided to call her in the morning.

When he got home, Rev. Johnson took the keys out the ignition and walked toward his front door. Once inside, he sat on the plastic covered couch and drifted off to sleep. He was awakening by the morning sun. He headed to the bathroom...

Looking at the **Golden Capri Hotel** information card, Rev. Johnson took another sip of his coffee and picked up the phone. He dialed the number on the card to get in contact with his daughter. He listened as the phone rung twice. On the third ring, a woman answered the phone, but she didn't sound like Lyla.

"Hello, Golden Capri Hotel. How may I help you?" asked the woman.

"Hello, Lyla? Is that you?" asked Rev. Johnson.

"No sorry. My name is Valerie. I am one of the desk attendant." said Valerie.

"Oh, hello Valerie. My name is Albert Johnson and I am trying to get into contact with my daughter, Lyla." said Rev. Johnson.

"Hello Mr. Johnson. This number only goes to the front desk. I can transfer you to your daughter's room. May I get your daughter's name?" asked Valerie.

"Yes, my daughter is Lyla. David had told me that she was staying there. Is that correct?" asked Rev. Johnson.

"Yes, she stays on the second floor. Would you like to be transfer now?" asked Valerie.

"Yes, I would." said Rev. Johnson.

Meanwhile, Lyla was in her room about to take a nice hot shower. She had been in the bed all day and needed to be refreshed. As she got her under garments, bath and dry towels, she stepped behind the shower curtain. Downstairs, Valerie tried to transfer the call to her room, but Lyla missed all three attempts. Valerie saw that she wasn't having any luck, so she asked the pastor if he would like to leave a message for her and he said "No. I'll try again some other time."

The reason why Rev. Johnson was hesitate to leave a message for his daughter, was because he thought that his daughter was still mad at him and wouldn't want to talk to him at all...

After getting out of the shower, Lyla saw the red light flashed on the phone. She had never missed a phone call before she wondered who could have called her. She walked to the closet and put on a black dress that she had hanging up and brushed her hair. She decided to asked the desk attendant downstairs, which would most likely be Valerie to find out who had called her. As she gathered her room key and cell phone, she headed downstairs to the lobby. Valerie was behind the desk. She was happy to see Lyla.

"Hey Valerie. I noticed some missed call on my phone. Could you tell me who that might have been?" asked Lyla.

"Hi Lyla. Of course, your father just came and called your phone looking for you. He told me that his name was Albert Johnson. I didn't know that Johnson was your last name?" asked Valerie.

"Yes. Johnson is my last name. Did he leave you a message or call back number for me?" asked Lyla.

"No. He said that he would try to call you back. He sounded very disappointed when he couldn't get in contact with you. Is everything all right?" asked Valerie.

"Yeah, everything is fine. I'm about to head back to my room. If my father calls again, just transfer the call. I should answer it this time," said Lyla leaving the room with a shocking expression on her face. She hadn't heard from him in a long time.

Chapter Forty

Nina was lonely. She sat on her maroon couch and stared at the ceiling. She hadn't heard from Benjamin in several months. The last thing that she heard about him was that he was locked away somewhere. He had got caught up in his drug hustle that now he was paying the price. Nina rubbed her stomach. She was all alone. She had followed her mother's footsteps and became a pregnant unwed woman. No ring, no husband, no support. Nina began to cry. She missed her friend, Lyla. Nina missed her company, her laughs, hugs, and her friendship.

David drove home, still thinking about Lyla. Why was it so difficult to get her out of his mind? He was deeply in love and there was no ignoring it. David decided to do something that would be very difficult for him. If time was what Lyla needed, then time was what he would give her with the help of the Lord. David really didn't want too, but he had no other choice. Lyla would continue to push him away until he gave her time to clear her mind. David could feel his heart ache. He would miss seeing her beautiful smile and pretty brown eyes, but he must do what was best for her and not for him.

He picked up the phone and dialed the number to the Golden Capri. He called the front desk and Valerie answered the phone. "Hello, Golden Capri Hotel. How may I help you?" said Valerie.

"Valerie, this is David. I am calling to let you know that I would not be at the hotel for a while. I have a lot of thinking to do and just need some time to be alone. I hope that you can understand." said David.

"Hello, David. I understand. Take as much time as you need. If ever you need someone to talk to both I and Joe is for you." said Valerie.

"Thank you. I really appreciate it." said David as he slowly hung up the phone. The last words that he heard from Valerie were you are...dial tone. He had hung up before Valerie could finish her words. David decided to be absent from the hotel for at least two weeks, that should give Lyla plenty of time. Well at least he hoped so.

Back at the hotel, Valerie hung up the phone with a sign expression on her face. She began to get a little worried. Meanwhile, Lyla stared at the phone in her room hoping her father would call. Now that she was attentive and ready to retrieve the phone, her father didn't call at all. Lyla really did miss her father. Lyla missed the breakfast conversations, his word of wisdom and his knowledge. She was so anticipated about his call that if given the actual chance to speak with him, she would be speechless. Lyla hadn't spoken to her father in about a year and they never had stayed in contact, so what would she say?

"Hello father..."or how about "Father, this is your daughter Lyla?" Both sounded so proper and out of context for her. Whenever she was given the chance to speak to her father, she would say the exact words that were in her heart, not only on her lips.

Rev. Johnson

Still at home, Rev. Johnson drunk his third cup of coffee before heading to the firm. He wore his corduroy slacks and a buttoned down collar shirt with the sleeves rolled up half way to his elbow on either side. On his left wrist, he put on his golden watch that magnetic clasped together and grabbed his firm's planner documented in a large binder and his car keys. As he left the house, his phone rung. He barely answered it, while being in a rush. But then stopped when he assumed that the call could be Lyla. "Hello, Lyla oh how I missed you..." said Rev. Johnson but stopped quickly when a man's voice was on the other end not his daughter.

"Pastor Johnson sorry to bother you, but I need your help again." said David.

"David? Hey son, what's going on with you? I was on my way out the door and how did you get my number?" asked Rev. Johnson.

"I found your number from the church directory. I have a confession to make: I love your daughter. I told myself that I would give her sometime at least two weeks to clear her mind, but I can't wait that long without seeing her. What should I do?" asked David.

"Pray about it, son. Ask the Lord to help you and guide you during this uncertain time." said Rev. Johnson. "I really do have to leave, if there is nothing else I can help you with." Again, he grabbed the binder and his car keys.

"Well there is one last question that I would like to ask you before you go, Reverend?" asked David.

"What's that, son?" asked Rev. Johnson.

"With your blessing, may I take your daughter Lyla Johnson hand in marriage?" asked David. Reverend Johnson dropped both the binder and his car keys on the floor. He wiped both ears to make sure that he heard Brother David correctly.

"Son, what did you say? It sounds like you are asking my daughter's hand for marriage?" asked Rev. Johnson.

"I am, Sir. It would be both an honor and a privilege to marry your daughter. I want her to be my wife and I want to be her husband." said David.

"Son, you sound as though you are completely serious about this. Are you sure this is what you want to do? You know marriage is no game, it is a covenant that has been ordained by God." said Rev. Johnson. "I don't want you rushing into something that you are not ready for."

"Reverend Johnson, I am completely ready for this. I love Lyla with all my heart and I do not want to spend my life with any other person except her." said David with sure confidence.

"Son, I have to go. I don't want to be late for work." said Rev. Johnson. He was still uncertain about this whole thing. To him, everything appeared to be going so fast and quickly. Did David even know Lyla well enough to marry her? Have they ever dated before? He had question after question and a young man who thought that he was ready.

"All right, Reverend. But would you please consider the request? I would really appreciate it" asked David, before hanging up the phone.

"Yes, I would son. I would consider the request." said Rev. Johnson. As he opened the car door to his Toyota to get inside, a thought went through his mind as he fastens his seatbelt. He wanted to make sure that David knew what he was getting himself into. Lyla being his daughter and only child, Rev. Johnson knew what made her happy and sad and her mood swings that she experienced. He wanted to be completely sure that David was the one for her. After putting his car in the ignition, he dialed the number that David dialed to contact him.

"Hello, son. I thought about your request and wanted to ask you a question before I gave you a response." said Rev. Johnson.

"Well, hello again. Rev. Johnson that was very fast. What is the question that you have for me?" asked David.

"Out of all the women that come in and out of church on Sundays and other services and those who are tenants at the hotel, what makes my daughter the only candidate for marriage? For surely, you see many beautiful women everywhere you go?" asked Rev. Johnson. Again, he was only asking David to see how sure he was about marrying Lyla.

"Yes, Reverend. You are absolutely right. I do see several gorgeous women at church and also at the hotel, but none compares to your daughter. With Lyla, it is very different. When I see all the other women, I only see the make-up and attires that they wear but not with Lyla. I see a genuine and kind woman, that has suffer with a few scars and bruises outwardly, but inwardly she is truly in love with the Lord, which is all I ever wanted in a woman. A woman who loves the Lord." said David. "Did I answer your question correctly?"

Again, Reverend Johnson was speechless to how well David responded. Surely, he was ready for her hand in marriage. His response was that of depth and truth. "Yes, son. Welcome to the family."

Chapter Forty-One

Lyla became annoyed. She just couldn't stare at the phone all day. She wondered if her father had forgotten about her. If so, this wouldn't be the first. After their argument that they had in the past, she lost all contact with him and not once did he ever called or looked for her. She was beginning to get mad all over again. She decided not to think about the past. As she stared at the phone, the time went by so quickly. Already, the time was a quarter to five. She figured that the lobby dining area should be serving food pretty soon.

She found out that tonight's meal was spaghetti and meatballs with a side of tossed salad, either rolls or white and wheat bread, and green beans or corn. She cannot wait to eat, she was stressed out that her father didn't call and just couldn't wait for this day to be over. She wondered how David was doing. She still couldn't forgive herself for being so rude to him.

When he got off the phone with Rev. Johnson, David felt at ease. He didn't know that asking his pastor for his daughter's hand in marriage would be both scaring and exhilarating. David didn't know if he wanted to cry or shout, but did know that he had to release his joy in some way. He had saved up about fifteen hundred to about two thousand dollars for an engagement ring. He had waited for this moment to come. Now the next task would be to find out what ring size did Lyla wore. He would have to ask Rev. Johnson to find that out.

About to pick up the phone to call Rev. Johnson, David stopped when he remembered that pastor said that he was busy. He decided to call back another time. Meantime, David stopped by Jared's, a jewelry store to just window shop for Lyla's ring. Once there, he found a ring that had Lyla's name all over it. As he pushed the door to walk inside, the glare of the ring sparkled grabbing his full attention. "May I help you?" asked the jewelry clerk.

"Yes you can. May I see that ring inside the display glass?" asked David, pointing specifically at the chosen beauty.

"This one, Sir?" asked the clerk.

"No, the ring right next to it. On my right and your left." said David.

"Oh, I see. You are talking about this beauty." said the clerk.

"Yes, that is the one. How much does it cost?" asked David.

"I am not for sure. Let me do a price scan. The price is about eighteen hundred dollars." says the clerk.

"Wow, well that does sound about right. The ring is such a beauty." said David.

"It sure is. So would that be cash or credit, Sir?" asked the clerk.

"Neither. I am not going to get it today, because I don't know my fiancé's ring size. This whole thing is pretty new to me." said David. "My father-in-law would have to come with me next time. Can you keep the ring for me? I can give you my name and my contact information." He spoke as though the ceremony had already taken place and Lyla was engaged to him. David was definitely sure of himself about this.

"I don't know, Sir. I would have to check with my manager to find out. If he agrees, how long do you think it would take for you to purchase it?" asked the clerk.

"I would try to be back as soon as possible. I would have to check with my father-in-law schedule." said David handing the ring back to the clerk. "Can you ask your manager before I go?"

"Yes, let me check to see if he is here." said the clerk. He headed toward the back room to the manager's office. To his surprise, the manager was there filing some documents. He knocked on the manager's door and asked if he could come in. His manager waved him in the office. The clerk asked the manager what David had asked him and quickly returned back to the front. "My manager said that he would try to keep the ring until Monday of next week. Would you be here before then?" asked the clerk.

"Yes. My father and I should be here before Monday." said David.

"Good. Then we would see you then. Bye, bye now." said the clerk.

Chapter Forty-Two

By the time Rev. Johnson got home, it was a quarter to seven. He had been at the stock firm all day. *I am so happy to see this place.* Reverend Johnson took off his shoes to let his toes breathe, for his feet been cramped inside all day. As he rested on the couch, he thought about his daughter again. He still didn't remember what him and Lyla were arguing about, but he did know that he missed talking and seeing his child.

Thinking about his daughter, he reached inside his wallet to find the card that had the hotel's information. After calling her twice and couldn't get through, he placed the card back inside his wallet. Heading toward the remote control on the living room table, the phone rung and the Reverend quickly picked it up. He thought that Lyla would be the one to call him, but the person it wind of being was David.

"Hello Lyla, I tried calling you…" said Rev. Johnson.

"Hi Reverend, this isn't Lyla. Did you ever get in contact with her?" asked David.

"No, I thought that this would have been her calling me, not you. Anyway, how are you doing this evening?" asked Rev. Johnson.

"I'm doing well. I just left Jared's not to long ago and found this beautiful engagement ring for Lyla." said David. "Speaking of the ring, do you know what size Lyla wears?"

"No I am not sure, but I am glad to know that you are taking a move on Son." said Rev. Johnson. "Are you really ready for this?"

"Yes, Reverend. I am ready." said David as he drove into the grocery's store parking lot. He had decided to stop by the store before going home. He wanted to pick up some more sugar and creamer for his lattes and get some additional things that he needed. Tonight, the store wasn't that all busy. There were only a few cars in the parking lot.

"Son, are you still there?" asked Rev. Johnson as he turned on the television set to see what was on. He flipped through the channels until he saw a familiar face caught by the police. The man looked like that wannabe gangster that Lyla use to date. *Lord, what was his name...uh, Fred, Steve...*

Reporter: Police found Benjamin Bentley and two of his other friends involved in a drug mafia which included two dangerous gang members...*Benjamin, the boy name was Benjamin. Good, I hope him and his buddies get locked up.* Reverend Johnson didn't like Benjamin. He knew that the boy was trouble from the start.

"Yes I am here." said David as he closed the car door. He debated if he would need a cart or not, while walking toward the store. Perhaps, a small hand basket would work out just fine for him. "Are you at home or at work?"

"I just made it home." said Rev. Johnson still thinking about the news. Grabbing a basket near the entrance, David headed to the aisle that had the coffee products. He looked above his head aisle five had the products, including the coffee roast in several kinds.

"Reverend Johnson, would you be free anytime this week? I would like for you to see the ring with me." asked David.

"Well I know that I don't have anything plan for Saturday. Would you like to go sometime in the morning?" asked Rev. Johnson.

"Yes, the morning should be fine. Is eleven o'clock good for you?" asked David.

"That should work for me. Should I meet you up there or we both going in one car?" asked Rev. Johnson.

"We can just meet each other up there. I went to the Jared's off of 27th Cornell, the one by the old Shells gas station." said David standing in the check-out line.

"I know where that is at. I would see you then. Have a good night, Son." said Rev. Johnson.

"You too, Reverend." said David grabbing his plastic bags and leaving the store. As he placed the bags in his truck, he figured out how to get Lyla's ring size without her knowing it. Maybe, he could ask Valerie to get it for him, but then he debated if he should even tell Valerie why he needed that information from Lyla in the first place, because he knew that she would want to know. David decided to pray about it first. *The Lord would work it out, eventually.*

Arriving home, he took the bags out of his truck and unlocked his front door. Reaching for a switch light, he turned on two at the same time and accidently turned on the ceiling fan. *Oh, leave it on* he decided and put his bags on the table. So far, everything was coming together. Rev. Johnson said that he would meet David at Jared's on Saturday to see the beautiful ring. David couldn't wait to see his expression. He hope that Rev. Johnson would love it as much as he did.

Saturday approached very quickly and David was so excited. He had a feeling that Rev. Johnson would love the ring and that the ring would go home with him today. As Rev. Johnson and David stood in line, Rev. Johnson thought that now was the best time to tell David about Lyla's past; how she was abused and beaten by her ex-boyfriend and might still be scarred from the pain. At first, he wasn't going to say anything at all just let the past be the past, but if David didn't know her past how would Lyla recover and David console her?

Rev. Johnson had prayed about it before and the Lord had told him to speak. Now was the time to be obedient and tell his soon to be son-in-law the truth. Surprisingly, David was willing to hear all that Rev. Johnson had to say and his response was: "Oh, I would be very gentle to her and of her past." Right then and there, David proved to be the chosen one for his daughter, Lyla.

Without trying to be absent from the hotel, David was gone for about two weeks for Lyla's ring preparation. After finding out the correct ring size from Valerie: size 7. David quickly found a pretty velvet case and tied a perfect bow. *There...*he said. *Perfect!*

Nina

Meanwhile, Nina decided if she should return back to the hotel to talk face to face with Lyla or stay home. Nina decided to leave and find her friend. Taking her dear time, she rubbed her stomach to feel the baby's feet. Just recently, she went to the doctor's office for her weekly check-ups and the doctor said that she and the baby were doing fine. Now she was both nervous and excited about the expectance. Nina made sure that she had her purse and car keys before leaving the house. As she drove her BMW, she thought of what words to say to Lyla when she saw her. She wanted to apologize to her without causing an argument, but didn't know how.

Deep down inside, she knew that Lyla wouldn't be too thrilled to see her, but she must at least try to make things right between them two. As Nina arrived at the hotel, she bumped into David again. He walked past her and headed directly to Lyla's room, but then suddenly stopped when he remembered the conversation that he had with Rev. Johnson about Lyla's pain. If she had been scarred, then surely Nina had too. At that very moment, David saw something in Nina that he hadn't saw before: a hopeless girl.

Before going to Lyla's room to see if she was there, David spoke to Nina. "Hi, do you remember me?" asked David. "I'd help you, well tried to before the altercation between you and Lyla happened."

"Oh, yes I do. Do you know if Lyla is here?" asked Nina.

"She should be, but I am not for sure." said David. "Nina, is everything all right between you and Lyla? It seems like you two use to be very close friends, now Lyla gets this disgusted expression when she sees you. How come?" asked David.

"Because I deserve it, David. I did something terribly wrong in the past and now I am reaping what I had sowed. I would tell you what I did, but it is to shameful to both think and talk about. David, just keep me in your prayers." said Nina.

"Whatever happened in the past is not too great for God to handle, Nina. We all have our short comings and flaws, so don't be too hard on yourself." said David. After saying this, he gave Nina a bear hug that made her smile.

"Thanks for cheering me up, David. I really needed that." said Nina.

"You are welcome," said David as he gently halted for Nina to stay behind.

Chapter Forty-Three

After talking to Nina, he told her to wait by the door while he spoke to Lyla first. Nina listened and stayed behind. As he knocked on Lyla's door, his heart beated fast. David never knew he could be so nervous. He knocked on the door again. Finally, she answered with a surprised look on her face. All this time, Lyla thought that David was upset with her that was why they haven't been seeing much of each other. But David reassured her that wasn't the case at all, he loved her.

"That's right, Lyla. I love you. I love your brown eyes, pretty smile, and good heart. Lyla, I understand that you have been hurt in the past and that you moved away to escape the pain, but only God has that ability to change our lives and move whatever obstacle that may stand in our way. Lyla, I prayed for this very moment and am pleased that God had sent you my way. From this day forward, I promise to love you with all my heart and soul. Lyla Star Johnson, will you marry me?"

David rested on one knee and brought out the velvet case and opened the box. Before Lyla stood a 22k sparkling silver style crest triple diamond ring. Lyla was speechless. Outside the door, Nina overheard the conversation and silently cried. Nina was so happy for Lyla. "So, what do you say Lyla?" asked David.

"Yes, David! The answer is yes!" said Lyla helping her fiancé to his feet. They kissed each other on the lips for the first time. David didn't forget about Nina outside. "Lyla, a friend of mine is outside and would like to see you. Would that be all right?" asked David.

"Of course. Any friend of yours is a friend of mine, let them in." said Lyla with a huge grin on her face. As Nina opened the door and walked inside, Lyla's grin quickly disappeared. "David, what is she doing here?" asked Lyla.

"Lyla, she is my friend and she wants to be yours too. Lyla, please hear her out. She wants to apologize for all the wrongs that she has done to you." said David as he grabbed Nina's hand to welcome her inside.

"Lyla, your fiancé is right. I am truly sorry for hurting you and betraying your trust. Lyla, if you choose to never forgive me I understand. I don't deserve your forgiveness." said Nina as tear began to roll down her cheeks. As Nina spoke, Lyla looked at David as he nodded his head to usher Lyla to go forward. Lyla took Nina's hand and looked her in the eyes.

"If the good Lord can bless me with a wonderful man, even after I have fallen short. Then surely, I can forgive an old friend of mine. Nina, I forgive you." said Lyla opening her arms to embrace her old friend again like she used to. After forgiving and having compassion for Nina, Lyla gave her another hug and felt the baby inside of her kicking away. "How many months are you?" asked Lyla.

"Eight and half months," said Nina as she rubbed her belly. She missed her old friend and was happy to have her back in her life again. David did right by us, to have allowed such a strange encounter of two former enemies. *Again, look at God.* After David made the proposal, he called Father Johnson and told him the good news.

"Congratulations!" said Father Johnson. What still awaited Lyla was the reconciliation of her father and the ultimate forgiveness for Benjamin. The first trial wouldn't be that hard to do, but to forgive Benjamin would be like placing hot coals on her head. How could she forgive him, when he didn't even apologize for his wrong doings?

He just did what he wanted to do, which was lie, cheat, and lie some more. David could sense Lyla getting mad all over again. "Lyla calm down. Let's take things one day at a time. Don't matter what happens, I am here with you. So you are not alone nor by yourself, but by forgiving your ex-boyfriend, you become free from any bondages or strongholds that he has over you. Lyla, until you forgive him, we could never truly love one another without some fault arising. Forgive Benjamin." said David.

Again, Lyla was speechless. Sometimes, she didn't know if she was speaking to her fiance or a ordain preacher, in a way he did sound like her father. She could tell that David had been under his divine teaching. "Even if I were to forgive him, where would I look first? Benjamin could be anyway for all I know." said Lyla.

"Earlier, when I spoke to father Johnson he told me where we might be able to find Mr. Benjamin." said David.

"Where?" asked both Nina and Lyla at the same time.

"You two would see soon. Just get in the car and I would take you two to the place where he is." said David. The two women were terrified. David had taken them to jail. "David, why are we here?" asked Lyla.

"This is where Benjamin is at. He is here in jail." said David. They all walked toward the guards to fill out the guest list.

"David, I don't like it here. Please let us leave now," said Nina, but honestly she couldn't wait to see Benjamin and tell him everything. Lyla, on the other hand, just wanted to say *apology accepted* and leave this place. David remained calm the whole way through as if being in this place didn't bother him at all. Finally, he said that the *prison ministry has helped him a lot*. Now everything made sense that was why he wasn't afraid at all.

Again, Lyla became hesitate about seeing Benjamin. It had been about a year or so, since Lyla last saw him and now that she had the chance to say how upset he made her, she wondered if she would have the courage to say anything.

"Lyla, are you all right?" asked David with much concern. "You have been quiet since we came here."

"David, I see what you are doing. But I don't think that I am ready to forgive my ex-boyfriend for all the pain that he caused me. Can we just leave, please?" asked Lyla. David could see how fearful she was about the whole situation, so he gently held her hand to assure her that he would be right next to her as she confronted her past. "David, do you think that I am strong to do this? I am not that strong girl that I use to be." said Lyla feeling more and more afraid as she approached the iron bars that separated her from her ex-boyfriend. While Lyla was scared, Nina was too as she tried to find the right words to tell Benjamin about her pregnancy. She figured that she was a big girl, she would just tell him. It shouldn't be that hard.

"Yes, Lyla I know that you are strong to do this. I would be right by your side." said David as they were escorted by one of the security guards to a cell.

"Hey, Ben! You got some company out here." shouted the security guard. David could see how this was going to turn out if the security guard continued to call out to Benjamin. David could sense some tension.

"We can take things from here." said David as the security guard stopped before saying any more words. The security guard looked David up and down, than slowly glanced at the two ladies with him. He stared deeply at Lyla. David noticed this and said "uh officer, you can leave now" and grabbed Lyla hand to indicate that she was his.

"Fifteen minutes...I am giving you only fifteen minutes to say whatever you need to say." said the security guard as he straightened out his black leather belt and waddled back to his station. Behind the bars, Benjamin looked beat and tired like he just came out of a fight. The fade that he once had has disappeared into a not badly afro cut and he now had a full beard. After the security guard had left, Benjamin turned around to see who his visitors were. Surprisingly, he smiled when he saw both Lyla and Nina together. Both of them were silent, but David spoke up first. "Hello, my name is David. I know we haven't met each other, but I am so glad to finally meet you." said David.

Benjamin looked David up and down, like the security guard had done before speaking. "I am honored. I see that you have come across two of my fair ladies." said Benjamin. David didn't get offended at all. Again, he looked at Lyla.

"Benjamin, my fiancé wants to say something to you." said David. Benjamin looked at Nina with a snarl on his face.

"All right. Go ahead." said Benjamin. David took Lyla's hand and led her before Benjamin. "All right, Lyla. Go ahead." This changed everything. Benjamin was sure that the chosen girl was Nina. Lyla took a deep breath.

"Benjamin Bentley, I forgive you. I forgive you for all the pain and hurt that you had caused me even though you have not apologized at all. I need to move on with my life. I can't continue to carry these burdens on my back." said Lyla with a sign of relief. David attended to Lyla's side.

"How do you feel? Any different?" asked David.

"Yes. I feel free!" said Lyla holding his hand. After Lyla spoke, Nina came forth and just told Benjamin flat out.

"I am pregnant and yes I am keeping the child." said Nina, giving Benjamin the snarl that he had gave her at first. Nina knew that raising their child alone would take a lot of work, but she was willing to try. David held her hand too, "you are not totally alone. Lyla and I are here to help you as well." Nina giave a sly smile before stepping back from the bars.

"Guard, I think we are done now. Thanks again." said David escorting the two ladies out.

Chapter Forty-Four

Leaving the prison, all three of them got back into David's car. Nina had been getting some badly contractions and believed that now was the due time. David rushed to the nearest hospital, which happened to be Wyckoff Heights Medical Center off on Division Ave. "We need a nurse immediately. I think my friend is about to go into labor!" said Lyla as they rush into the double doors entrance. A nurse attended at Nina's side, but asked if David could wait outside of the delivery room, while Lyla stayed inside to help Nina proceed with the procedures. Outside, David could hear Nina pushing and grasping for air, then pushed again, while Lyla tried to console her. "You're doing well. Take deep breaths now." said Lyla as the gripped of Nina's hand became tighter for her.

After the delivery of the new baby boy weighting at about seven pounds and eleven ounces, the nurse asked Nina "if she wants the man that is outside to come in?

"Yes, let David come in to see my son." said Nina. The nurse went outside and told David to come inside the room. As Nina held her son, Nina eyes sparkled and Lyla saw a sense of joy that she hadn't seen from Nina ever. When the nurse asked Nina what she would name her son, she said: Benji Lyvid Carter, incorporating both Lyla and David names together to form his middle name. She had asked if they would like to be Benji's god parents and David quickly said yes. From this everyone laughed including the nurse and other medical doctors.

Nina stayed overnight at the hospital, these were the doctor orders. David and Lyla stayed by her side and spend the night as well. Before leaving the hospital, Lyla softly kissed Nina's forehead with her lips to assure her that everything would be all right. David kissed her forehead and Lyla's forehead too. There was so much love shared in the room. David was happy to see everyone coming together. Leaving the hospital, David took Lyla back to the hotel to got dressed for church.

Again, he asked Lyla if she wanted to go to church with him and surprisingly she said: yes. "Yes, I would go to church with you," Lyla said with no hesitation. She was ready to make things right with her father. She figured that would be the only place he might be, in the sanctuary. At the hotel, Lyla wore a pair of black slacks with a creamy white blouse. Outside, David waited until Lyla was fully dressed before heading to his house. They both rode together. At home, David wore some black corduroys with a white buttoned down shirt.

Overall, Lyla felt extremely blessed. She was blessed with a wonderful man that really loved her for her and was definitely a gift from the Lord. He enjoyed long walks in the park and especially reading God's Word, the Holy Bible. He was all that she ever wanted and more; he felt the same way. When they arrived to church, Lyla squeezed David's hand as they walked inside the sanctuary. It had been such a long time, since Lyla had been there. "You look so nervous, Lyla. Everything would be all right. Remember, this is your church family not strangers. They all would be happy to see you." said David.

And again, David was correct. As they both walked into the church, the members were all smiling and greeting them as they passed everyone. Wow. Lyla never felt so loved by many people. As they walked closer to the pulpit, Rev. Johnson was interrupted by her presence. He called out her name: "Lyla! Sisters and brothers please stand on your feet and welcome back my daughter." said Rev. Johnson. Slowly, the Lord worked everything out. So far, Lyla had forgiven both Nina and Benjamin for the wrong they had done to her. She has befriended Nina again and felt a huge weigh of burdens lifted off of shoulders, when she forgave the man that caused her much pain. Now, the only thing that awaited Lyla was reconciliation with her father, Rev. Johnson.

Everyone applauded as David and Lyla took their seat at the front row, Rev. Johnson asked the couple if either one of them wanted to say something. David shook his head No, but Lyla slowly raised her hand up in the air. "Yes, daughter?" asked Rev. Johnson.

"I would like to say something, Father. Many of you might remember me from long ago as the woman who once preached and taught God's message. The woman that use to be on fire for the Lord, well I am still that woman. I just had lost my way off of God's gracious path. Today, I have come back home to be in His presence. Being away, I have found several heartaches, headaches, and hardships in my life and now I just need a new beginning." said Lyla looking around the congregation for support.

The church was completely quiet, when out of nowhere Eddie the choir director began to sing a song that welcomed everyone to join:

Amazing Grace. How Sweet the Sound. That Saved a Wrench Like Me. I Once Was Lost But Now I'm Found Was Blind but Now I See.

Epilogue

Walking around Prospect Park with her lovely fiancé holding his hand and laughing makes Lyla feel a sense of joy and happiness that she hasn't felt in a long time. David is a wonderful man that loves Lyla with all his heart. He accepts both her inner as well as her outer beauty and is simply amazing. He admires the way her wavy hair falls down behind her back, the way her lips curled whenever she'd smiled, revealing her pretty dimples and her pure skin.

He loves and respects Lyla for who she is a unique and intelligent woman that deserves to be treated like a queen and cherish forever. She doesn't have to change or pretend to be someone she's not. She's perfect the way she is, whenever David says it. It is mid-December in Brooklyn and the snow has covered the streets like a white quilt. Parked cars has lined up along the asphalt of the city, leaving a trail of wheels in the snow. But not a trail of betrayal and hurt that use to linger around in Lyla's heart, when she was in a bad relationship, base off of lies and confusion.

Meeting David has mended up the open wounds of hurt in Lyla's heart and allows the strength of love and forgiveness to release the inner-joy within. David has given back all that Lyla has lost, including her puppies: Charlie and Miley and so much more. Although, she is happy now, she hasn't always been so happy. But one thing is for sure, Lyla has found deliverance in the Son and the shackles have been broken.

www.ingramcontent.com/pod-product-compliance
Lightning Source LLC
LaVergne TN
LVHW091552060526
838200LV00036B/801